*You have th*

"What's you_____nan asked.

Sam's stomach twisted into a tight, painful knot. "Samuel Bardin," he answered.

Officer Griane stepped forward, holding out a pair of gray steel handcuffs. "Samuel Bardin, you are under arrest. You have the right to remain silent. Anything you say can and will be held against you in a court of law. You have the right to an attorney. . . ."

As the officer continued to recite Sam his Miranda rights, Sam felt the cold metal of the handcuffs close around his wrists. The policeman's voice became indistinguishable from the roaring in Sam's ears. He was being carted off to jail—like father, like son.

Don't miss any books in this hot new series:

café

*#1 Love Bytes*
*#2 I'll Have What He's Having*
*#3 Make Mine to Go*
*#4 Flavor of the Day*

Available from ARCHWAY Paperbacks

For orders other than by individual consumers, Pocket Books grants a discount on the purchase of **10 or more** copies of single titles for special markets or premium use. For further details, please write to the Vice-President of Special Markets, Pocket Books, 1633 Broadway, New York, NY 10019-6785, 8th Floor.

For information on how individual consumers can place orders, please write to Mail Order Department, Simon & Schuster Inc., 200 Old Tappan Road, Old Tappan, NJ 07675.

# @café

# FLAVOR OF THE DAY

## by
## Elizabeth Craft

INDIANAPOLIS MARION CO.

PUBLIC LIBRARY

**AN ARCHWAY PAPERBACK**
Published by POCKET BOOKS
New York   London   Toronto   Sydney   Tokyo   Singapore

The sale of this book without its cover is unauthorized. If you purchased this book without a cover, you should be aware that it was reported to the publisher as "unsold and destroyed." Neither the author nor the publisher has received payment for the sale of this "stripped book."

This book is a work of fiction. Names, characters, places, and incidents are either products of the author's imagination or are used fictitiously. Any resemblance to actual events or locales or persons, living or dead, is entirely coincidental.

AN ARCHWAY PAPERBACK *Original*

An Archway Paperback published by
POCKET BOOKS, a division of Simon & Schuster Inc.
1230 Avenue of the Americas, New York, NY 10020

Produced by Daniel Weiss Associates, Inc., New York

Copyright © 1998 by Daniel Weiss Associates, Inc., and Elizabeth Craft
Cover art copyright © 1998 by Daniel Weiss Associates, Inc.

All rights reserved, including the right to reproduce this book or portions thereof in any form whatsoever. For information address Daniel Weiss Associates, Inc., 33 West 17th Street, New York, NY 10011, or Pocket Books, 1230 Avenue of the Americas, New York, NY 10020.

ISBN: 0-671-00448-4

First Archway Paperback printing March 1998

10  9  8  7  6  5  4  3  2  1

AN ARCHWAY PAPERBACK and colophon are registered trademarks of Simon & Schuster Inc.

Cover photos taken at DRIP, New York, NY.

Printed in the U.S.A.

IL 7+

*For the team at DWAI:*
*Thanks for all your help.*

**BACK**

**FORWARD**

**HOME**

**STOP**

LINK: [                                        ]

## Tanya's Star Scape:
## Your Astrological Guide
## Scorpio
## (October 24–November 22)

Passionate Scorpios are in for an extra-bumpy ride this month. Just when you thought you had your life semi-under control, you find yourself spinning down a black hole. All I can tell you is to hang in there—maybe the force of the earth's gravity will find you and pull you back. Eventually.

**Mood:** They say "let a smile be your umbrella," but you, poor Scorpio, are finding out even the biggest umbrella doesn't do much good in a hurricane. Remember: Real men (and women) aren't afraid to let loose with a good cry every once in a while.

**Love:** Disaster. I don't think I need to say more on this subject.

**Friends:** Thank goodness for friends. Keep your friends close this month. You're going to need them. But don't be surprised if someone trusted lets you down. We're all human, and even the best of friends blows it sometimes.

**Lucky number:** 15

Late Tuesday night Sam Bardin pushed open the door of the van Lentons' forest green Mercedes. He hopped out before Natalie could bring the car to a stop. Right now he felt as if he could have jumped off a moving train and landed on his feet.

"Sam! Wait!" Natalie yelled. She slammed on the brakes, and the Mercedes screeched to a halt.

"Meet us inside," he said to her. The back passenger-side door opened, and Eddie jumped out.

"She's gonna be okay," Eddie whispered. "She has to be."

Sam took a moment to study his little brother's pale face. Eddie was only fifteen, but at the moment he looked much older. His dark eyes looked tired, and his forehead was creased with worry.

Sam placed a hand on his brother's shoulder. "Mom will pull through, Eddie." He took a deep breath, fighting back tears. "I know she will."

Natalie was leaning toward the passenger-side window. "I'll park the car and get inside as soon as I can," she assured Sam.

Natalie's voice was calm and

**ONE**

1

steady, but Sam knew that she was terrified. During the fifteen-minute drive to San Francisco Memorial Hospital she'd gripped the steering wheel so tightly that her knuckles had turned white. Sam had stared at her hands the whole ride, trying in vain not to relive the memory of two paramedics loading his mother's motionless body into the back of an ambulance.

"Hurry," Sam urged. He needed Natalie by his side when he heard the news—whatever the news turned out to be.

Sam stood still, watching the taillights of the Mercedes shine in the dark night as Natalie pulled into the visitors' parking lot. Just seconds ago he'd felt as if he couldn't get inside the huge hospital doors fast enough. Now he wished that he could spend the next few hours standing out here. Sam didn't feel ready to face the doctors and nurses or the harsh white light of the waiting room.

"Sam, come *on*," Eddie ordered. He pulled on the sleeve of Sam's blue rugby shirt. "Don't just *stand* there."

Sam blinked. The taillights had disappeared. It was time for him to take charge. "Let's go." He forced his feet to move toward the entrance of the emergency room.

Inside the hospital the reality of what was happening seemed to sink in for the first time. Somewhere nearby his mother was lying on a gurney with several doctors leaning over her, determining whether she would live or die.

"Excuse me," Sam said to a stern-looking nurse who sat behind a long white desk in the center of the room. "I'm Sam Bardin. My mother was brought in here a few minutes ago." He heard the fear creeping into his voice and took a deep breath.

The nurse looked up from a clipboard she was studying. Her dark eyebrows were thin sharp lines that highlighted her flat brown eyes. "Bardin?" she asked. "What's the spelling?"

Her nasally voice sounded to Sam like fingernails on a chalkboard. He read the name tag attached to her starched white uniform: Jane Stanton. At least her name seemed relatively unthreatening.

Sam swallowed his rising frustration. Ms. Jane Stanton was his link to his mom. *"B-a-r-d-i-n,"* Sam said slowly. "Margaret Bardin."

The nurse typed the letters on a keyboard attached to her giant computer. "Uh-huh . . ."

"What?" Eddie demanded. "What is it?"

Nurse Stanton glanced at Eddie. Was it Sam's imagination, or did the woman's expression seem more sympathetic now? Oh, God—from this ice cube sympathy was probably a death knell. "Your mother is with Dr. Rodriguez right now. The doctor will be out in a minute to tell you how she's doing."

Sam groaned. "Can't you tell us *anything?*"

The nurse shook her head. "I'm sorry. You'll have to wait for the doctor."

"She's dead," Eddie moaned. "I know it. She's dead."

Sam placed one hand on each of Eddie's shoulders. "Eddie, stay calm. The nurse didn't say anything—maybe Mom is totally fine."

Damn. Sam was too young to play dad to his little brother. Why wasn't their father here? Talk about a rhetorical question. Joseph Bardin wasn't here because he was stuck in the slammer.

"Let's sit down, Eddie." It was the most comforting thing to say he could think of.

Sam guided his brother to a row of black vinyl seats that had seen better days. He tossed aside a *Good Housekeeping* magazine from 1996 and sank onto the rock hard seat cushions. Eddie perched two chairs down the row and stared toward the nurse station, where Jane Stanton had returned to what was apparently some urgent typing.

Sam closed his eyes and silently cursed his father. None of this would be happening right now if Joseph Bardin had an ounce of integrity. Officially he had been convicted of income tax invasion—but Sam knew his father's transgressions were more serious than that. And Sam would never forgive him. Mr. Bardin's absence had driven Mrs. Bardin over some kind of invisible cliff. For months she had been drinking too much. More recently she had taken to replacing warm milk at bedtime with a concoction of Valium and who knew what else. Tonight she had overdosed.

"Sam!" Natalie's voice seemed a million miles away, but when Sam opened his eyes, he saw that she was standing right in front of him. "Have you heard anything? Is she going to be okay?"

He shook his head. "We don't know anything yet, Nat."

She slipped into the seat beside him and placed her arm around his shoulders. Natalie pulled him close, and Sam allowed his head to drop against her shoulder. He could smell the strawberry scent of shampoo and feel the silky texture of her long dark hair against his cheek. "She'll get through this, Sam." Natalie raised one hand and ran her fingers lightly through his short dark hair.

Sam sighed deeply. He wished he could stay in the safe haven of Natalie's arms forever.

"I think that's the doctor," Eddie screeched. "He's coming toward us!"

Sam tore himself from Natalie's embrace and popped up from the row of seats. "Dr. Rodriguez?" he asked a middle-aged man with longish black hair and a white lab coat.

The doctor nodded. "Are you Mrs. Bardin's children?" he asked.

Sam nodded. "Yes." He wanted to ask how his mother was, but the words wouldn't come out.

Dr. Rodriguez glanced around the waiting room. "Is your father here?"

"No," Sam barked. "Just tell us how she is."

"Your mother ingested a large amount of alcohol

and prescription drugs," the doctor said slowly. "She's stabilized now, but we don't know if she's going to make it through the night."

Through the loud roaring in his ears Sam heard Natalie's gasp and Eddie's anguished moan. The truth was out. His mother might die—and there wasn't a damn thing he could do about it.

"Natalie." Her name sounded so good coming out of his mouth that Dylan O'Connor decided to say it again. "Natalie . . ." He smiled at himself in the rearview mirror. "Natalie!"

This time Dylan had yelled her name. Goofy? Yes. But he felt so *good* that he didn't care if he was acting like the biggest dork on the planet. At least Dylan *had* felt good, but now Natalie was late for their date—really late.

Dylan glanced at his watch for the tenth time in what must have been only a few minutes. It was now almost one o'clock in the morning. Okay, so Natalie was supposed to meet him an hour ago. She could have gotten stuck in traffic, or been car jacked (not a comforting notion), or run out of gas.

"So what if she's late?" Dylan muttered. Girls were always late. She was probably spending extra time on her hair or something. He grimaced. It was the *or something* that was making his stomach churn.

Maybe Natalie was with Sam.

No, that wasn't possible. Natalie's note had been clear—she was breaking up with Sam because she was in love with Dylan. Period. Dylan leaned back and stuck his right hand into the pocket of his faded Levi's. The folded piece of notebook paper was still there. He pulled it out, unfolded it, and held the paper up so that he could read the words in the light of the streetlamp.

*Dear Dylan,*

*I'm not sure exactly what I want to say to you in this note.* [Blah, blah, blah. Skip to the important part.] *I'm going to break up with Sam tonight.* [Etc., etc.] *I love Sam, and he'll always be one of my best friends. But I felt something when we kissed that I've never felt before.* [And so on. And so on.] *I'll be parked at The Verandah Pier at midnight.*

*Always,*
*Nat*

All right, the note didn't explicitly state that Natalie was in love with Dylan. But he knew in his heart that she cared as much about him as he did about her. The unforgettable kiss they had shared on their way home from Portland had proved that to him. All Dylan had to do was find Natalie, and she would tell him face-to-face exactly what the note had meant.

Dylan started the engine of the 1972 yellow Oldsmobile Cutlass convertible he had purchased a few weeks ago. Sam had convinced him to follow his heart and buy the convertible rather than follow his mind, which had told him to buy a minivan. Sam—his best friend. Dylan fought back a wave of guilt. His best friend was going through one of the toughest times of his life, and Dylan was plotting to steal his girlfriend. Well, he wasn't exactly *plotting*. Things between him and Natalie had just . . . happened.

This late at night the streets of San Francisco were nearly deserted. Dylan breathed in the cool night air as he steered the car toward Natalie's house. Part of him wanted to turn on the radio and find some sappy Whitney Houston ballad to sing along to. But he didn't think he should do anything else to jinx himself. He had spent the last couple of hours in a state of delirium, positive that tonight everything between him and Natalie was finally going to come together. Since she hadn't shown up at the pier at the appointed time, caution was definitely called for. Yes, he was cautiously optimistic. Or optimistically pessimistic. One of the two.

Dylan turned onto Lyon Street and slowed the Oldsmobile to a stop in front of the van Lentons' large Victorian house. A few lights were on, but the place was more or less dark. Ringing the doorbell was out of the question—his nerves were plenty jangled without the prospect of having Natalie's somewhat intimidating father answer the door in the middle of the night.

He shut off the engine. *Please be home, Nat.* Dylan jumped over the side of the convertible and sprinted across the street. At the curb he bent over and picked up a handful of loose gravel. Had Romeo felt something like this as he wooed Juliet from underneath her balcony? *Natalie, Natalie, wherefore art thou, Natalie?* Or whatever the line was.

Dylan walked across the van Lentons' dew-covered front lawn and stopped beneath Natalie's second-floor bedroom window. The first pebble hit the side of the house. Dylan took a step back, adjusted his aim, and threw another piece of gravel. This time he was rewarded with a satisfying ping against the window. *One, one thousand; two, two thousand.* Dylan detected no movement inside the house. He tossed another pebble, then another. Unless Natalie had been knocked unconscious, she would *have* to hear the sounds against her window.

"Is there a reason you're defacing the side of our house?" Mia van Lenton's voice was typically mocking.

Dylan turned around, feeling blood rush to his face as he looked at Natalie's nineteen-year-old sister. "Hi, Mia."

She arched one eyebrow. "Dylan."

Natalie's older sister looked like a model—she

*was* a model. Mia's long auburn hair was perpetually shiny, and her dark red lips were always glued in a seductive pout. But Mia's overt good looks had never moved Dylan. He preferred Natalie's soft, warm allure.

"I'm, uh, looking for Natalie," Dylan stammered. "I didn't want to wake anyone up."

Mia shrugged. "Natalie's not here. I haven't seen her since this afternoon."

"Oh." What now? Natalie wasn't home. Dylan had been caught throwing pebbles at her window like a cheesy love struck character in a bad movie. If he had even an ounce of pride, Dylan knew he would slink to his car and drive off into the night.

*Go away,* Dylan willed Mia. She stood rooted to her spot, her arms crossed in front of her chest. "Well . . . good night," Dylan said hopefully.

Mia shook her head, laughing. "I'm not going to walk back into that house and let you sit in your car for God knows how long while you wait for my errant little sister to return," she said.

She had read his mind. Dylan felt himself blushing even more in the darkness. Did he look *that* pathetic? "I'll just, uh, head home," Dylan said. He hadn't felt this humiliated since Mrs. Karp had intercepted his love note to Trina Walters and read it to his entire seventh-grade English class.

Mia grinned. "You can wait inside, Dylan."

He let out a sigh of relief. "Thanks."

Dylan let the small handful of pebbles fall to the grass and followed Mia toward the van Lentons' front door.

"I assume you're not here on official café business," Mia said as they climbed the short flight of steps that led to the porch.

"Uh, no. I mean, yes." Dylan had no intention of expanding his statement. Spilling his guts to his ex-girlfriend Tanya Childes about his secret passion for Natalie had been bad enough. The whole world didn't need to know that he was hopelessly in love with his best friend's girl.

"Whatever." Mia opened the front door and stepped aside. "Don't worry about waking up my dad," she said, reading Dylan's mind once again. "He's been asleep for, like, hours."

Dylan nodded absently. Now that he was actually inside the house, he wasn't sure this was such a great plan. Maybe Natalie hadn't written that note at all. Maybe Tanya had forged it as some kind of twisted prank. It was entirely possible that when Natalie finally showed up at the house, she would have Sam in tow. What would Dylan say then?

*Come home, Nat,* he willed her. *Alone.* He headed for the living room, repeating the silent prayer. He had to find out exactly how Natalie felt about him. And he had to find out tonight.

### Blue's Sound Bytes:
### One Girl's Observations About
### Life, Love, and Other Atrocities

Hey, all. Can we talk about parents for a minute? I mean, I just don't get why moms and dads—especially moms—take such pleasure in torturing their daughters. Don't get me wrong. I love my mother tons (really, Mom!). But sometimes I think she's convinced that she picked up the wrong bassinet at the hospital.

"I'm so proud of you," she says. "I just want you to be happy." Okay, okay. Wonderful, encouraging things for a parental unit to utter. But then she totally *undermines* the statements by picking apart each and every little thing I do wrong. "Did I raise you to live like a slob?" she'll ask. As if not washing one stupid cereal bowl is right up there with murder on the list of the seven deadly sins.

Here's my favorite I'm-not-really-proud-of-you-even-though-I-say-I-am comment: "Blue, you could be pretty if you would just do something with that hair, stand up straighter, and put on two pounds of makeup." I happen to like my hair—it's got personality. And I don't *want* to look like Tammy Faye. As far as I'm concerned, the feminist movement could stand to step up the pace so that we could move past this whole red lips, rosy cheeks, long black eyelashes thing.

I'd just like to know how my mother would like it if I ate one of her dinners and said, "Gee, Mom, the fried chicken is really good. If only all the fat and cholesterol you packed into this five-thousand-calorie dinner wasn't going to clog my arteries and kill me by age twenty-six." Yeah, maybe I'll say that at dinner tonight. Or not.

Blue felt the edge of the cash register digging into the small of her back. Every part of her body was suddenly extraordinarily sensitive—especially her lips. She leaned forward, pressing her full weight against Jason's strong chest. His lips captured hers yet again, sending fresh tingles down her spine.

Blue's heart hammered wildly in her chest. Sensations that she had never experienced—but had read about in Cosmopolitan—coursed through her veins. She felt like . . . a woman. Blue tilted back her head so that she could gaze into Jason's eyes.

But the eyes didn't belong to Jason—his were piercing deep blue while these were a warm, gold-flecked hazel. Christian's eyes. Blue blinked.

"Kiss me." His voice was low and soft—but whose voice was it?

A pair of strong, firm hands rested on either side of her hips, burning through the denim of her cutoff shorts. Blue slid her hands up his back and cupped her hands around his chiseled face. "Jason . . . ," she whispered. "Christian . . ."

Once again Blue pulled back and blinked several more times. Jason's face came into focus. She absorbed

**T W O**

*the sight of his longish shiny brown hair and dark red lips. But when Blue blinked again, the hair became a light brown that was silky to the touch. This was Christian.*

*She closed her eyes and puckered her lips. She was desperate to feel full, soft lips against hers, no matter who they belonged to. Now that these feelings had been awoken, Blue was experiencing a hunger she had never imagined.*

Sara Jane (aka Blue) O'Connor opened her eyes. Except for the glow-in-the-dark star stickers she had placed on her ceiling, her room was black. Wow—what a dream. She'd had dreams about guys before. She had even dreamed once that she and Jason Kirk were making out on a beach outside of the city. But never—never—had it felt so real. Tanya and Natalie had talked about raging hormones and bones turning to liquid and heart-hammering kisses, but Blue had always assumed her friends were more or less full of it. Now she realized they weren't.

Blue's pulse was still racing as she leaned over and glanced at the digital clock she kept on the floor next to her mattress. 1:14 A.M. Man, she felt wide-awake. And sort of . . . restless. Blue sighed heavily. Less than a month ago she never had annoying problems like insomnia.

Life had been direct, simple, and generally satisfying. She had spent all of her sophomore year at

Alta Vista High School ditching classes and goofing off with her best friend, Jason. And then there had been the ideal summer. She and Jason both worked at her older brother, Dylan's, café, where they continued an amusing pattern of accomplishing the least amount of work with the maximum amount of flair. Yes, Blue and Jason had been the perfect noncouple, in league with greats like Felix and Oscar, Laverne and Shirley, and Abbott and Costello.

But all of that had been before The Fall—the label Blue had given to Matthew Chance's fateful party. Blue kicked off the thin cotton sheet that covered her body and rose from her mattress. If she wasn't going to sleep, she might as well do something productive . . . like what?

She flopped onto her favorite beanbag chair and gazed out the window. If only she and Jason hadn't been accidentally set up on that stupid, horrible date. Until the night of The Fall, Blue had insisted that she had no time or interest in romance. Why, *why* had she caved so easily when Tanya and Natalie wheedled her into going on a blind date? And why had the date turned out to be Jason? Once Blue had looked at Jason through the eyes of a girl who was supposed to be on a so-called date, everything had changed.

And now Jason was going out with that awful girl Celia. The mere thought of her made Blue want to pull the stuffing out of her beanbag chair. The girl had the looks of a piranha and the personality of a toothpaste model. Man, she was bad.

*Don't think about Jason and Celia,* she commanded herself. She had moved on. She was going to go out with Christian Sands, the cute folk singer she had met on one of Tanya's girl-bonding outings. Maybe. Maybe she wasn't going to date anyone.

Either way, she was going to make absolutely sure that she never had another dream about kissing Jason Kirk.

Natalie's hazel eyes burned with exhaustion as she fished in her backpack for her wallet. "Just a sec," she told the cabdriver.

He glanced at her in his rearview mirror. "Tough night, huh?"

Natalie nodded. "Tough doesn't even begin to describe it." Finally she located her wallet. Natalie pulled out ten crumpled one-dollar bills and thrust them toward the driver. "Life just doesn't make sense sometimes," she commented, to herself as much as to the cabby.

The driver took the money. "In this world the only thing you can count on is death and taxes," he answered.

Natalie sighed. *Death.* The word echoed in her mind. She slid out of the taxi and shut the door quietly behind her. "Bye," Natalie mouthed to the driver as he pulled away.

Her eyelids felt as if they weighed about ninety pounds each. All she wanted to do was climb into bed and sleep until it was time for her to show up at work tomorrow afternoon. As she hoisted her backpack up over her left shoulder her eyes fell on a car parked across the street.

"Oh, my God," she whispered. That wasn't just any car. It was Dylan's. "Damn."

She had forgotten all about Dylan. And the note. He had absolutely no idea that Sam's mother had overdosed tonight. As far as Dylan knew, Natalie had simply stood him up. How could she have forgotten about Dylan—the guy she loved?

Natalie squinted and peered at the convertible. Unless Dylan was hiding underneath the dashboard, there was no one inside. She turned back toward the house and jogged up the brick path that led to the front door. If Dylan was there . . . jeez, she had a lot to explain.

Natalie opened the door slowly and slipped into the quiet house. She let her backpack fall to the hardwood floor with a soft thud and took two steps toward the living room. There he was, sprawled out on the van Lentons' long black leather couch, his arms crossed on top of his broad chest. The mere sight of him caused her breath to catch in her throat. Dylan was so . . . beautiful.

*I'm sorry, Dylan. I'm sorry that tonight isn't going to end the way both of us wanted.* Natalie tiptoed over to the sofa. Dylan's soft, light brown hair was sticking out in a hundred different directions, and his full red lips were parted in sleep. Natalie felt her breath quicken as she stared at his chest rising and falling in the rhythm of sleep. He was irresistible.

As much as she wanted to throw herself in Dylan's arms and spill a torrent of pent-up emotions, Natalie knew she couldn't allow it. Sam needed her now more than ever. She couldn't let him down. Breaking up with Sam while his mother held on to her life by a wispy thread just wasn't an option.

Natalie perched on the edge of the couch and tapped Dylan lightly on the shoulder. "Dylan," she whispered. "It's me."

His eyelids fluttered but remained closed. "Dylan," she whispered again, a little louder this time. He was completely out—Natalie suspected that he would sleep all night on the sofa if she let him.

She wiggled a little deeper into the couch and leaned over so that her face was directly above his. Natalie had never noticed how long Dylan's lashes were. One little kiss on the cheek probably wouldn't do any permanent damage to her karma scale.

*I love you,* Natalie told him silently. She brought her lips to Dylan's perfectly sculpted cheekbone. Once. And then twice. And then once on the other side. Finally she forced herself to sit up more or less straight again.

Dylan's eyes opened. "Nat." A slow, seductive smile played across his face. "I thought I'd never find you."

Natalie laughed. "I think *I* found *you.*" Her voice was low and husky.

"I'm glad you did." Dylan didn't bother to sit up on the couch. Instead he held out both his arms, then placed one hand on either side of Natalie's face. He brought her head closer and closer until their lips were just millimeters apart.

Natalie knew that she should resist. Her brain was screaming at her to pull away and tell Dylan about everything that had happened tonight. But her heart . . . her heart wouldn't listen. Dylan brought his lips to hers.

And then they were kissing. A shock traveled from Natalie's lips to the tips of her toes, and any ideas about kindness, decency, and loyalty were quashed beneath a mountain of unbelievable sensations.

"Dylan," she moaned. For this moment Natalie was connected to the guy she loved. And she wished the moment would never end.

*This is great,* Tanya Childes told herself. *Jackson Whatever-he's-called is totally hot, and his lips are soft and so strong.* She pulled Jackson closer and slid her hands down his back, letting her fingers rest lightly on his lean hips.

*Get real.* This was the most boring make-out session in the history of make-out sessions. Finally she pulled away.

"I better go," she murmured, trying to muster a certain amount of regret in her voice. "I think I hear my mom walking around inside."

Jackson didn't let go of her waist, but he did move his head a few inches away from her face. Yes, the guy was indisputably gorgeous. Bright blue eyes, a long blond ponytail, and high, chiseled cheekbones—Tanya knew they made a striking couple. The contrast of her ebony skin and black curly hair and Jackson's fair good looks would probably turn dozens of heads if they were to walk down Haight Street together. Nope, there was nothing wrong with that picture. Okay, there *was* one tiny, minuscule, unfortunate detail. Jackson What's-his-name wasn't Major Johnson— beautiful, dark, muscular Major.

"I don't hear anything," Jackson said. He turned his head and glanced through the small window next to the Childeses' front door. "It looks totally dark in there."

Jackson leaned forward again. Tanya pressed her head back against the front door. She simply didn't think she was up for another wet, sloppy kiss. "Uh, my mom is really sneaky. She can tiptoe around so silently that you wouldn't even know she was there. And she, uh, doesn't need a lot of light to get around the house." Okay, Tanya sounded like a complete idiot.

"Maybe you should ask her if I can come inside for a while," Jackson whispered. "Saying good night now would be a tragedy."

*And continuing to kiss you would be a comedy,* Tanya answered silently. "Uh, I don't think that's such a good idea," she said, trying to look disap-

pointed. "The thing is, my mom's kind of a tyrant."
Excuses, excuses—she knew a million of them.
"And my dad, he's like a drill sergeant."

"Really?" Jackson asked. He was squinting—although Tanya couldn't tell whether his expression
indicated fear, confusion, or disbelief.

She nodded vigorously. "Yeah. I mean, I'm not
even allowed to date."

"You're not?"

"No," she said emphatically. "My parents think
I'm over at Natalie's right now. If they see you here,
it could be bad news—very bad news."

Jackson dropped his arms and took a couple of
steps backward. "Maybe I *should* be going. I don't
want to, uh, get you in trouble or anything."

Tanya sighed. "That probably *is* the best idea."

Jackson squeezed her hand. "Give me a call sometime. I mean, if your mom and dad say it's okay."

Tanya nodded. "I will. Definitely." *Not.* She waved
at Jackson as he stumbled down the front steps.

"Good-bye, Jackson," she whispered. Tanya
sighed deeply. *Another one bites the dust.*

Tomorrow she would find a brand-new guy. A guy
who would make her feel weak in the knees when
she kissed him and who she would dream about at
night. In short, a guy who made her forget Major.

BACK

FORWARD

HOME

STOP

LINK: [                              ]

## Jason Kirk Tells It Like It Is

Has anyone noticed the way a bad day tends to get worse? I woke up the other day and discovered that my alarm clock had somehow malfunctioned during the night. I was, like, already an hour late for work. Okay, no big deal. I'm late for work all the time, anyway. Right?

So I put on a pair of *really* dirty jeans and a smelly T-shirt from the large pile on the floor of my bedroom and race downstairs to wolf down a bowl of Lucky Charms. Unfortunately I'm going down the stairs so fast that I trip on the second-to-last step, fall, and split open my bottom lip. While I'm waiting for the bleeding to stop, I scream about a million words that aren't fit to repeat here.

When I finally get to @café, my boss (you know who you are) berates me in front of a roomful of customers, one of whom happens to be the girl I'm dating. So I look like a total weenie, but there's nothing I can do since I *am* late and a generally horrible employee.

Two hours pass in a relatively harmless manner. I'm serving coffee, wiping down tables, smiling at the country club girls who come into the café, giggling and squealing like a bunch of lab rats caught in a maze. And then—bang. I burn my hand on our wacky, totally unpredictable espresso machine. While I'm jumping up and down and crying out in pain, I accidentally knock over an entire row of coffee mugs. The enormous crash is followed by more of my boss yelling at me like I'm a total idiot. Which, of course, I am.

When I finally arrive home after my miserable day, my dad informs me that I left the front door wide open when I left the house in the morning. He says he's tempted to ground me, but he's decided living with my own stupidity is punishment enough.

Needless to say, I spent the rest of the evening in my room—stashed away from the many terrible things that happen when I venture out.

*Your mother is going to make it.* Dr. Rodriguez's words echoed in Sam's mind as he wandered the corridors of San Francisco Memorial Hospital. *She was very lucky—this time.* This time. The ominous overtones in the doctor's statement had not been subtle. Sam's mother could have died tonight.

The hospital seemed to be closing in on him. White walls. White-tiled floors. White ceilings. Sam felt as if he had walked into an alternative universe in which colors didn't exist. San Francisco Memorial was unrelenting in its decor, as were the sight of uniformed doctors and nurses and the smell of whatever it was they used to keep the place sanitary. Sam had been pointed in the direction of the coffee machine, but he felt as if he had taken a dozen turns since he had set off in search of caffeine.

Sam stopped in front of a door marked Lounge. This place was probably set aside for doctors, but at this time of night he doubted that anyone was going to be a stickler for details. He opened the door and poked his head inside. Aha. Sitting

**THREE**

atop a card table was a half-full pot of coffee. He ducked into the room and headed straight for the source of the much needed caffeine.

"Hi."

Sam's eyes scanned the small room. A petite girl with long light brown braids and wire-rimmed glasses was sitting on a gray metal chair next to an enormous coffee urn. She was wearing faded jeans and a bright yellow T-shirt that had Camp Thunderbird emblazoned across the front. "Hi," he answered.

She held up a small foam cup. "Looking for java?"

He nodded. "I need about a dozen of *those*," he said, nodding toward her coffee cup. He walked to the urn and poured himself a cup of what looked like little more than muddy brown water.

"I'm Hallie Barnett," the girl said.

"Sam Bardin." He sat down on an identical gray metal chair and took a sip of the lukewarm coffee. "What is this stuff?"

Hallie grinned. "You're obviously not a regular here."

Sam raised his eyebrows. "What do you mean—a regular?"

Her smile faded. "Let's just say that I while away more hours than I care to admit sulking over this bad coffee."

Until now Sam had only thought about his own reasons for being at the hospital. But he knew there was plenty of heartbreak to go around at San Francisco Memorial. "Uh, why are you here so much?" he asked.

"My dad has diabetes," Hallie answered. "Over the last year his condition has gotten pretty bad."

"Oh." Sam didn't know what else to say.

"What about you?" Hallie asked. "What brings you to this lovely place?"

A lump formed in Sam's throat, and his mouth suddenly felt dry. Part of him wanted to tell Hallie that his mother had been in a car wreck or that his little brother had broken his arm. But Hallie's blue eyes were warm and understanding behind the lenses of her glasses, and he was so worn out by the lies and secrecy within his family that he didn't think he could pull off being The Good Son.

"My mom overdosed on pills and booze," he said harshly. "She almost died."

Hallie nodded. "That's rough."

"Tell me about it." Sam felt bitter tears threaten to spill from his eyes. He blinked rapidly and forced himself to focus on a diagram of the heart that was tacked above the coffee urn.

Hallie cleared her throat. "Want to talk about it?" she asked.

He shook his head. "Not really."

She nodded again. "I'll tell you what—I'll give you my sad and pathetic story, which will surely make you feel better about your own current lot in life."

"Shoot," Sam said. He took another sip of the coffee and tilted the chair back on two legs.

"My mom died two years ago," Hallie started. "Breast cancer."

"I'm sorry," Sam said. "I can't even imagine what that would be like."

"No, you can't," Hallie answered. She crossed her arms over her chest. "After Mom died, my dad lost all interest in life."

Sam could understand *that*. His mother had more or less checked out of planet Earth since his dad had been sent to prison.

"Anyway, he used to monitor his diabetes really well," Hallie continued. "But since my mom's been gone, he's had a horrible diet and totally quit exercising. Ergo, he's been in and out of the hospital for months now." She paused. "If he doesn't make some pretty radical lifestyle changes, he's going to die."

"And you'll be alone," Sam said.

"Yep." Hallie's voice wasn't shaking, and her expression was as calm as it had been when he walked into the room. Sam was awed by her ability to remain detached from the fact that her family was a complete mess.

"My dad is in jail," Sam said. She was the first stranger he had shared this information with.

Hallie sighed. "So much for *Leave It to Beaver* and *Father Knows Best*."

Sam laughed. "My life is definitely closer to *Married . . . With Children*."

*"I'm* going to be cast in a new Fox show called *Party of One,"* Hallie said. "Those orphans don't know how lucky they are to have brothers and sisters."

"We're a pretty pitiful duo," Sam commented.

"At least neither of us is lying on some hospital bed attached to a bunch of tubes and heart monitors."

"Good point." Sam raised his cup of coffee. "To our health."

Hallie tapped her cup against his. "Amen, brother."

Sam actually managed a smile as he brought the cup to his lips. Everything in his life sucked—but his mother wasn't going to die, and he had made a new friend.

And then there was Natalie—she had been right beside him during those unbearable hours of waiting to find out whether his mother was going to live or die.

The silver linings were there. He just had to work hard to find them.

Natalie was drowning in an ocean of pleasure. Dylan's soft, full lips had melted into hers, and their kiss was going on and on and on. His hands slid up and down her back, sending shivers down her spine. Her own hands wandered across Dylan's broad chest, his muscular shoulders, the nape of his neck.

*Stop.* From somewhere far away the word worked its way into her consciousness. "Stop!" Natalie said, aloud this time.

Dylan ended the kiss abruptly. "What?" he asked. "What's wrong? Did I hurt you?"

His electric blue eyes were so filled with concern that Natalie felt a fresh wave of love wash over her. "No, of course not."

He sighed. "For a second there I thought that I didn't know the strength of my own lips." Dylan grinned, and Natalie couldn't help but notice the way his eyes seemed to shine from within.

Natalie took a deep breath. She knew what she was about to tell Dylan was going to wipe the smile off his face. But she couldn't wait any longer to deliver the bad news. Technically their kiss had been an act of cheating on Sam.

"Sam's mother overdosed tonight," Natalie blurted. "She almost died."

Dylan's face fell. "Oh . . . is she . . . ?"

"She's in a bad way—a really bad way."

Dylan ran his hands back and forth over the top of his head, a gesture Natalie had seen thousands of times during the many years of their friendship. She knew what it meant—he was worried. "Man . . . poor Sam."

Natalie nodded. "I went to the houseboat tonight to tell him . . . you know."

"To break up with him," Dylan supplied.

"Right." Natalie could still see the red flash of

the sirens lighting up the brisk, dark night. "The paramedics were loading her into the ambulance when I got there."

"How is Sam taking it?" Dylan asked. "Is he a wreck?"

Natalie nodded. "Pretty much. He blames himself for not nagging his mom more about all the prescription drugs she's been taking since his dad has been gone."

"So what happens next?"

Natalie shrugged. "I really don't know." She remembered the doctor's frightening words—addiction, crisis, death. "She'll be in the hospital for a while . . . and then . . . I just don't know."

Dr. Rodriguez had allowed Sam and Eddie to peek in at their mother. Natalie had hung back, not wanting to intrude on such an intimate family moment. But Sam had clasped her hand and urged her forward. He had needed her strength.

"You can't break up with Sam," Dylan said. "Not now."

"No." Natalie had known that Dylan would want her to stick by Sam in his time of need.

Dylan shifted his position on the sofa so that his and Natalie's bodies were no longer touching. He folded his hands in his lap and bit his lip. After a few moments Dylan glanced up and gazed into her eyes. "Your note meant everything to me, Nat."

Natalie swallowed the huge lump that had formed in her throat. "Every word came straight from my heart." She knew she sounded like a Hallmark card, but she didn't care.

"But Sam needs you right now," Dylan said softly. "And he needs me."

"Yeah." Natalie stared at Dylan's long dark lashes. This was why she loved him. Dylan would never sacrifice integrity and character for his own pleasure.

"So what are we going to do?" Dylan asked. "Should we pretend like none of this . . . stuff . . . between us ever happened?"

Natalie shook her head. "I don't think that's possible."

"Me neither." Dylan reached for her hand and laced his fingers between hers. "I've waited so long to tell you how I really feel . . . and now I feel like it's wrong for us even to be having this conversation."

Natalie resisted the temptation to move closer to Dylan on the couch. She had made her decision to stay with Sam the moment she had seen his ashen face tonight. The raw need in his eyes had pulled at her heart, and she had vowed to herself that she would see him through this.

"Maybe we *can* have this conversation the way we want to . . . someday," Natalie whispered. "But I don't know when that time is going to come."

"This is so hard—one of the hardest things I've ever faced," Dylan said quietly. "But compared to what Sam is going through, it's nothing."

Natalie forced herself to look away from

Dylan's lips. She could still feel their touch. "I think we should avoid being alone together," Natalie choked out. "If I'm going to be with Sam, I've got to be there—one hundred percent."

Dylan nodded. "From here on out, we're just friends."

"Good friends," Natalie said.

"*Very* good friends." Dylan was staring at her in a way that made Natalie feel as if she was in the middle of the kind of dream that made her blush in the morning.

"You should, uh, probably go home now," Natalie squeaked.

He stood up. "I'll tell Sam that you called to let me know what happened with his mom," he said. "There's no point in mentioning that we saw each other tonight."

Their first lie. Would it be the last? "Good plan," Natalie agreed.

"Uh, don't see me to the door," Dylan said gruffly. "I don't think I could deal with a good-bye tonight."

Natalie didn't answer. She simply closed her eyes and listened to the sound of Dylan's retreating footsteps. The front door opened, then clicked softly shut.

*I love you, Dylan.* She hadn't said the words aloud tonight . . . it wouldn't have been right. "I love you."

31

# Natalie Spouts Off
## (In Praise of) Dr. Laura Schlessinger

For all of you who are totally out of it, let me explain who Dr. Laura is. She's one of those radio psychologists—like Frazier Crane—who provides endless hours of entertainment by letting us listen in while other people moan and groan about their problems.

Dr. Laura has gotten a lot of pretty bad press. Liberally minded people (of which I am one, by the way) think the good doctor is *way* too harsh to her callers. She denounces any couple who make the decision to live together without being married (gasp!), she's totally pro-life, and she doesn't think *anyone* should get a divorce (except maybe if one spouse is getting beaten silly by the other). Don't even ask her about premarital sex—you'll get the kind of lecture that you'd think only Mama could deliver.

So when some poor sap dials up Dr. Laura and complains that his kids don't like their new twenty-five-year-old peroxide blond stepmother, she generally responds by telling the guy that he's a selfish jerk who deserves whatever misery his kids lay on. And if a young girl is pregnant, Dr. Laura points out that she never should have put herself in a position to *get* pregnant, so it's said girl's obligation to buck up to the consequences.

But Dr. Laura has a lot of really great stuff to say. The thing is, Dr. Laura tells her callers to take control of their own lives. She tells them to stand up for what's right and not worry about offending people who think it's always better to be polite than to speak the truth.

You might decide you don't like Dr. Laura and her constant nagging. But listen to her a few times. I promise, she'll at least give you a lot to think about.

"Dude, I can't tell you how much I love the engine of your Olds," Sam said Wednesday afternoon. "The thing is a time bomb."

Dylan looked up from underneath the hood of his yellow convertible. "Why do you love the fact that my new used car is suffering from aging pains?" he asked. "I hate it."

Sam looked at the shiny new spark plug that was sitting in the palm of his hand. "Working on your car is something normal, something *real*. Unlike everything else in my life, your car has an ultimately finite number of problems that I can solve, given enough time."

"I see." Dylan ducked his head back under the hood of the car. "I didn't realize that anything in this world had a 'finite' number of problems."

Sam sat down on one of the milk crates he had dragged out from the alley behind @café. "Don't tell me that the ever positive Dylan O'Connor is feeling a bit bummed about the world at large."

F O U R

Dylan grunted. "If I'm your definition of positive, you're in a hell of a lot of a worse place than I thought you were."

Sam picked up the liter of lemon-freeze Gatorade he had bought from the deli on the corner and took a long swig. He had been feeling so lousy for so long that it had never occurred to him that other people didn't wake up singing "Zippity Doo Da" (or whatever that cloying Disney song was called).

"Talk to me, Dylan." Sam took another gulp of the Gatorade. "Just because my dad's a jailbird and my mom's an addict—hey, that's no reason I can't provide an ear for my best bud."

Dylan reached for a wrench. "You really need to do something about that dark sense of humor, Bardin. It's unhealthy."

Sam laughed. "If I can't point out the absurdity that makes up my family unit, who can?"

"Hopefully no one." Dylan tossed aside the wrench and grabbed an already greasy rag.

"You're avoiding the issue," Sam pointed out. "Instead of talking about your own demented self, you're steering the conversation back in my sorry direction."

Dylan backed away from the car and sat down on another one of the milk crates. "Hey, tell me what you want to know. I'm an open book, as they say."

Sam bit his lip. This was one of those times when the natural male-bonding process (which consisted mostly of spitting and talking about the relative merits of the butts of various girls) was in serious danger of being impeded. He and Dylan were about to cross the bridge between a good-natured insult fest and a meaningful dialogue. A big sign that said Proceed with Caution flashed in Sam's mind.

"I'm just saying that you seem sort of . . . lost," Sam said.

Dylan reached for the bottle of Gatorade. "I'm not lost, man. I'm just concentrating on work right now. I guess too much work makes Dylan a dull boy . . . or something."

Sam didn't credit himself with having a lot of perception when it came to the feelings of others. He could easily walk around in a self-involved fog twenty-four hours a day. But he was picking up a distinct signal from Dylan.

"You're lonely, aren't you?" Sam asked. "You live all alone in that tiny apartment, work fifteen hours a day, and don't touch girls with a ten-foot pole," he continued without giving his best friend a chance to respond to his thesis point. "Yeah, you're *lonely*."

"Don't be stupid," Dylan said gruffly. "I'm not lonely . . . I'm just alone."

Sam saw all the pieces falling into place. Up

until the time when Sam started to date Natalie, he had hung out with Dylan all the time. Now Sam spent most of his free time watching movies and cuddling (for lack of a more dignified word) with the girl he loved. Dylan felt dissed. Duh!

"I think there's more to it," Sam said. "I think you're suffering from a lack of meaningful companionship."

Dylan snorted. "Give me a break, Sam."

"I don't *make* the truth—I just speak it." Sam studied the emotions that flickered through Dylan's eyes.

Yep. His friend was definitely holding something back. And Sam suspected that he knew exactly what it was. Dylan was jealous of the fact that Sam—the guy who had never dated one girl for more than three days at a time—had actually landed in a real relationship. Dylan, Mr. Loyal to the Death, needed some lovin' for himself.

Sam pushed himself off the milk crate and stepped over the car. "I have diagnosed the problem, O'Connor, and I intend to do something about it."

Dylan rolled his eyes. "Let's resume the pattern of our normal friendship," he said. "You take care of your business, and I'll take care of mine."

Sam shrugged. "Whatever you say." But once his face was hidden behind the hood of the Olds, he smiled.

Sam was going to put on his so-called thinking cap and help Dylan out of this funk. If Sam owed anyone a little kick in the butt, it was Dylan. Sam's best friend had always been there for him, and he absolutely intended to return the favor.

"Love is a battlefield," Tanya announced to Blue and Natalie. "At least that's what Pat Benatar says."

Blue glanced up from the oversize coffee mug that she was washing. "Love is a joke," she answered.

"Love is tragic," Natalie said. She was lying on the blue crushed velvet sofa that was pushed against one wall of @café.

Blue set down the mug a little harder than was necessary. "Can we *please* talk about something besides love for once?" Sometimes Natalie and Tanya made her want to puke.

"Did anyone give table three their check?" Natalie asked. "They just walked out the door."

Tanya slid out of the booth she had been sitting in and sprinted to the door. "Hey, losers!" she screamed. "Pay up!"

Natalie rose and walked to the plate glass window that lined the front of the café. "They're gone," she said flatly.

"Oops," Tanya said. "I guess that one's coming out of my pocket." She slouched back over to the booth and sat down.

Blue abandoned her post at the large sink behind the counter. If Natalie and Tanya weren't going to do any actual work, then why should she bust her butt washing dirty coffee mugs? The fact that her older brother owned @café didn't make her feel compelled to perform any more manual labor than was strictly necessary. Thank goodness for what was known as The Midafternoon Lull. The three girls at table three had constituted the last of the customers.

"I guess it's pointless to ask if they left a tip," Natalie commented. Then she yawned so widely that Blue thought she could probably take a filling inventory of the inside of Natalie's mouth.

Blue plopped into the latest addition to the café—a genuine La-Z-Boy that Dylan had bought for fifty dollars from a retired couple who were moving to a condominium complex in Tucson, Arizona. "Do you guys know anything about dream analysis?" she asked. "I mean, besides the thing that if you dream you die, that means you really are going to die."

"I think I need a new hobby," Tanya said from the booth. She swung her legs up onto the table and crossed her ankles. Not for the first time Blue found herself envying Tanya's long, well-muscled calves. "I heard that a lot of cute guys enroll in ceramics classes."

"I wonder if Sam minds that I'm not with him right now," Natalie said. "I mean, I was there this morning . . . but still."

Apparently no one was interested in discussing Blue's dream. Which was probably for the best, considering the fact that she had no intention of disclosing the fact that she spent half of last night in an alternate universe in which she was making out with both Jason and Christian.

"Dylan is with him, Nat," Blue answered, prying her thoughts away from last night's dream. "I'm sure Sam is fine. At least, as fine as he can be in this situation."

"Eddie and Sam are solid guys," Tanya commented. "Now that they know their mom is in trouble, I'm sure they'll do whatever it takes to help her get better."

Natalie sighed. "I guess you're right. . . . I just feel so guilty."

"Guilty?" Tanya asked. "Why do you feel guilty?"

"Uh, never mind," Natalie said. "Um, Blue, what were you saying about dream analysis?"

"Nothing," Blue answered. For almost a minute no one said anything. Blue used the period of silence to perform a deep breathing exercise. Breath in, one, two, three. Breath out, one, two, three. Breath in—

"Has either of you thought about going skydiving sometime?" Tanya asked. "I saw this *Road Rules* rerun where the entire cast jumped out of this really small plane. The pilot was hot with a capital *H*."

"What happened to your undying love for Major?" Natalie asked, stifling another yawn. "Don't tell me you've forgotten about him already."

"Major is in love with another girl," Tanya announced suddenly. Blue noted a weird cracking sound in her voice. Very un-Tanya. "He never cared about me at all."

"Come on, T.," Natalie said. "You know that's not true."

Blue's jaw dropped as she saw a tear work its way down Tanya's cheek. Blue had seen Tanya Childes rant and rave like a lunatic. She had seen her laugh so hard that she actually popped a button on a pair of shorts. And she had seen her pout with such style that Natalie had once suggested Tanya apply for a job as a professional spoiled brat. But Blue had *never* seen Tanya cry.

"It *is* true," Tanya insisted. "I saw him hugging her the other day. And then I called his apartment, and she answered the phone." The tears were really flowing now—Tanya never did anything halfway.

"Did Major *tell* you he had another girl-friend?" Blue asked. She knew Tanya tended toward the dramatic. It was entirely possible that she had concocted this entire theory after watching some girl complain about her cheating boyfriend on *Jenny Jones*.

"He didn't *have* to tell me," Tanya said. "I have eyes."

"Maybe you should talk to Major about this," Natalie suggested. "You're the one who's always telling us we shouldn't be afraid to face confrontation."

Tanya sighed, slumping lower into the booth. "He told me he didn't want a relation-ship . . . but he was lying. Major just doesn't want a relationship with *me*."

Blue hoped with all her heart that she never fell in love. Sixteen years of experience had taught her that love led to nothing but bad skin and ridiculous behavior. Look at Jason. Since he had met Celia Dalton, he had turned into a rude, inconsiderate jerk. Sort of.

Tanya sat up straight again. There was a dark gleam in her eyes that made Blue wary—Tanya looked like a girl who was forming a very bad plan. "Blue, call Major's house and see if *she* answers."

"I refuse to be a party to your obsessive-compulsive behavior," Blue said. Enough was enough.

Tanya arched an eyebrow—her trademark

gesture. "You're the one who just told me to deal with this problem once and for all."

"*I'll* do it," Natalie shouted. "*Jeez.*" She stomped over to the battered telephone that was attached to the wall next to the cash register.

Tanya rose slowly from the booth and followed. Natalie picked up the receiver, and Tanya punched in (really punched, as if she were poking out someone's eyeballs) the digits of Major's telephone number.

Blue imagined herself calling Jason's house to see if he was with a girl. She would die before she would submit to such humiliation. Of course, that wasn't the same thing. Tanya had it bad for Major, whereas Blue and Jason were just friends. If anything, Blue would be calling Christian Sands's house. Not that she would ever do that, either . . .

"It's ringing," Natalie hissed. Tanya looked as if she had swallowed a bowling ball.

"Is Maja there?" Natalie said in the worst southern accent Blue had ever heard.

A moment later Natalie covered the receiver with her hand. "He's there!" she whispered loudly to Tanya. "What should I do?"

"Hang up!" Tanya screamed.

Natalie slammed down the phone. "You should have asked if the refrigerator was running," Blue called.

"Was it her?" Tanya asked.

Natalie didn't have to answer. Even someone as dense as Blue in the matter of interpersonal human relationships could see by Natalie's expression that the answer to Tanya's question was a resounding, unfortunate yes.

"I'm going to kill him," Tanya declared. "First I'm going to torture him, then I'm going to kill him."

Suddenly a fresh round of tears started to pour from Tanya's eyes. "No, first I'm going to bawl. Then I'm going to torture him. And *then* I'm going to kill him."

Blue grimaced. Major Johnson and his mystery girl had absolutely no idea what the rest of the afternoon held for them. For the first time in weeks Blue felt that her own life was more or less in order. Tanya, on the other hand, was spinning out of control.

"Joseph?" Mrs. Bardin's voice was barely a whisper.

Sam looked up from the *Details* magazine that Tanya had dropped by on her way to work. He had read the same article four times, and he still didn't understand exactly why George Clooney was determined not to get remarried. Information simply wasn't processing through his brain at a normal rate of speed.

"It's me, Mom." He pushed himself off the black vinyl chair in the corner of his mother's semiprivate room and walked to the edge of her bed.

She smiled. "Sam."

"Do you remember where you are?" he asked. His mother had been drifting in and out of sleep for the past fifteen hours, and Sam wasn't sure how alert she had been in her moments of consciousness.

Her eyes clouded over, and she sighed heavily. "I'm in the hospital." She paused for several seconds. "And Joe isn't here. He's in jail."

Sam reached out and touched his mother's hand. She still looked so frail—her ivory skin was white as a ghost, her dark hair limp around her face. Sam had the uncomfortable feeling that she could go into cardiac arrest at any moment, although Dr. Rodriguez had assured Sam that Mrs. Bardin would be fine . . . as long as she didn't do a repeat performance with the pills and alcohol.

"I guess it's all coming back to you, huh?" He wondered if she had any idea how frightened he and Eddie had been. Sam had finally convinced his little brother to go home and sleep for a few hours—there was no point in both of them staying at the hospital.

"I remember passing out in the kitchen," she said slowly. "And then there were all these faces around me. . . . The doctor came in this morning and said that I almost died."

"That's right," Sam said.

"Sam, I'm so sorry. . . . I'm so ashamed." She pulled her hand away from his and covered her eyes. "I don't deserve to be a mother."

Sam had tried to prepare himself for this moment. But the reality of a face-to-face confrontation with his post-overdose mother was even more painful than he had imagined. Suddenly he felt more like a parent than a son.

So much had changed during the last few months. The huge house in which Sam had grown up had been the first thing to go. Mr. Bardin's enormous legal costs had forced them to sell the mansion and move into the small houseboat that had once been used for guests. Mrs. Bardin had traded in her new Lexus for a Honda Civic, and Sam had sold his BMW and bought a used motorcycle. And then his mother's friends had fallen away one by one.

"Don't blame yourself, Mom," Sam said quietly. "Eddie and I love you—all we want is for you to get better."

"Better," she echoed. "How can anything get better? Your dad is in prison, your mom is a useless, pathetic human being—"

"Don't say that!" Sam interrupted. "There's

nothing useless *or* pathetic about you. We're just going through a rough patch."

Mrs. Bardin removed her hand from her eyes and clasped Sam's forearm. "Nothing like this is ever going to happen again, Sam."

"No, it's not," he said firmly. "As soon as Dr. Rodriguez gives the okay, you're going to get out of here and go straight to a place where you can take care of your . . . problem."

He glanced around the sterile hospital room as he waited for her to absorb the news. The other bed was empty, for which Sam was grateful. He didn't like to think of his elegant, refined mother bunking with some possibly deranged soul who was suffering from a bad case of withdrawal—or who knew what else.

"Place? What kind of place?" Her voice was heavy with panic. "I want to go home—to the houseboat."

Sam shook his head. "You're going to a place called Hillbrook, Mom. It's a rehab center."

"No!" she yelled. "I don't need any kind of rehab. And I want to be at *home*, where I can take care of you and Eddie."

*Be firm, Sam. You can do it.* The time for gentle, loving support had passed. Sam needed to lay down the law. "In case you hadn't noticed, you're in no position to take care of us right now," he said. Sam forced himself to ignore his mother's tortured expression. "You've

46

got to take care of yourself. Eddie and I will manage."

Mrs. Bardin was silent for what felt like an eternity. "I'm so tired, Sam," she said finally. "I'm too tired to fight you."

A lone tear rolled down his cheek. It was the first he had actually allowed himself to shed since this nightmare had begun. "We're here for you, Mom," he said. "We're going to get through this—as a family."

# Tanya on the Subject of . . .
## The Late Princess Diana

Where to start on this subject? Let's see. . . . First of all, let me say that yes, Princess Diana's untimely death was a tragedy. The woman was only thirty-six years old, and she had two young sons who are going to be seriously bumming without the presence of their mother in their lives.

And I'm not going to lie. Even I, the queen of cynicism, shed a tear when Elton John performed his revamped version of <u>Candle in the Wind.</u> But let's look at this situation realistically, folks.

Princess Di was a product of the media. Yeah, she was hounded by paparazzi. Yeah, those freelance tabloid photographers are the scum of the earth. But Diana played the press big time. She wanted to be photographed. She used the press to lash out at Prince Charles and the queen. Like many celebrities, Princess Di wanted to have it both ways. She wanted all the publicity in the world when she looked good and none when she looked bad.

Diana, Princess of Wales, was a nice woman who did a lot of good for charity. But there are people in our very own country who devote their lives to public service—without the benefit of Chanel suits and tangos with John Travolta at the White House. I mean, I appreciate the fact that Diana kissed a man who was suffering from AIDS. She showed the world that was an okay thing to do. But let's not forget the people who tend to the very messy business of caring for diseased and disadvantaged people on a day-to-day basis. They're the *real* kings and queens of hearts.

Tanya tapped her newly manicured fingernails against the wheel of her mother's white Ford Taurus. She had spent the last forty-five minutes of her shift applying bronze-colored polish to her painfully bitten nails—much to the dismay of Dylan, who had returned to his establishment only to find the place in a state of sad disarray.

"All right, *chiquita,* show yourself," Tanya said aloud, her eyes glued to the front door of Major Johnson's apartment building. "I know you're in there."

Tanya switched on the car battery so that she could listen to the radio. Stakeouts were a necessary part of life—but tedious. She flipped through the AM stations, searching for something that would take her mind off the unpleasant task at hand. Tanya stopped turning the dial when she heard the soothing voice of Dr. Joy Brown, a feel-good pop psychologist who had a million answers for how women could get their husbands to put a little romance back into the marriage.

Some people visited psychics, some went to church, some consulted tarot cards. Tanya listened to talk show psychologists. As far as she could tell, most problems could be resolved between a commercial for Ovaltine and news at the hour. At the moment Dr. Joy was assuring a young mother that the sky wouldn't fall if she left her baby with Grandma for a couple of hours so that said young mother could go on a much needed dinner date with her husband.

"Aha!" The mystery girl had just exited Major's apartment building. Tanya turned down the radio and slouched low in her seat. Man, the girl was perky. She literally had *bounce* in her step. Sickening. Tanya counted silently to ten, waiting for Miss Thang to turn the corner. By nine and a half she was gone. Tanya opened the driver's-side door and stepped out of the car. She looked up and down the block to make sure that The Girl hadn't decided she couldn't stand to be without Major for five seconds after all. *Coast clear.*

Tanya's heart pounded in her chest as she jogged to the front door of the building. She held her breath as she pressed the buzzer for Major's apartment. What if he wasn't home? What if he wouldn't let her in? The door clicked open.

*I never want to see you again. I love you . . . please don't let me go. Tell me who the floozy is.* There was no great opening line. She'd have to wing it. By the time Tanya had climbed the long flight of stairs that led to Major's apartment, her pounding heart was accompanied by a layer of sweat over her face and neck. Beautiful.

*Ring the bell,* she commanded herself. Instead Tanya knocked—lightly. She quickly smoothed her somewhat wrinkled white miniskirt and took a deep, shaky breath. The door opened a couple of inches, and time seemed to stand still.

"Tanya!" Major didn't open the door any wider. He just stood there. "I didn't expect you."

She tried to smirk but managed something closer to a snarl. "I bet you didn't."

The way Major's loose khaki pants hung around his hips literally made Tanya's mouth water. He was soooo beautiful. Men weren't supposed to be this gorgeous. Mother Nature had seriously bungled when she gave Major those incredibly long black eyelashes and finely chiseled cheekbones.

"Uh, now isn't the greatest time," Major said. Apparently he wasn't bothered by the fact that they hadn't spoken for over two days. So much for the sexy kiss she usually received as a hello.

"I saw you with her," Tanya said abruptly. She had thought she would feel better once the words were out. She had been very, very wrong.

His face registered no change of expression. "You saw me with who?" he asked. "When?"

"Don't play dumb, Major." Tanya put her hands on her hips and gave him her best ice queen glare.

"I'm not playing anything," he answered. "I'm simply trying to figure out what the hell you're talking about."

"I hate you!" Tanya shouted. *I love you! Please tell me you love me!*

"I think we need to talk," Major said quietly—sort of the way her dad would utter those words after he discovered that she had accidentally stayed out until two o'clock in the morning.

Major took a few steps backward and opened the door so that she could go inside. Tanya knew she should stay out in the hallway, where she wouldn't be surrounded by Major's aura, but something compelled her to enter.

Tanya walked into the apartment and scanned the living room. Piles of books, magazines, and newspapers littered the floor and the large coffee table. There were also several socks strewn about the room . . . so far, so good. All of this was evidence of a male-only environment. Major had two testosterone-pumped guys for roommates—neither of whom shared his neat-freak sensibilities.

And then Tanya saw it. A pink scrunchie was lying on top of the TV set. There was also an incriminating copy of *Cosmopolitan* sitting next to the telephone. The girl obviously felt comfortable in Major's apartment. Tanya had certainly never left any of her girlie items lying around. Of course, Tanya had only actually been in the apartment twice, despite the fact that she had made something of a nonpaying career out of sitting in a car in front of the building.

"Tanya?" Major's voice broke into her thoughts. "Are you going to say anything?"

She tore her eyes away from the scrunchie. "When were you planning to tell me about your live-in girlfriend?" she asked.

"I assume you're talking about Faith." Major didn't even sound apologetic. Or panicked. Or anything at all except mildly irritated.

"Of course, I'm talking about Faith." At least she thought she was talking about Faith. Man, what a stupid name.

Major leaned against the wall and gave her one of his totally unnerving gazes. "You're upset."

Did the guy live to torture her? "*Yes*, I'm upset. I'm—"

"Tanya, I have two things to say to you." He sounded like a high school principal. How did a guy with so much sex appeal and charm manage to be so totally infuriating?

"I'm listening." Her knees were shaking.

"First of all, Faith has nothing to do with you and me." He sounded so sure of himself—there wasn't a trace of guilt or remorse in his voice.

"I disagree." There. She could be as blunt as he could.

He shrugged. "I've never lied to you, Tanya. If I tell you that Faith has nothing to do with us, I mean it."

"What's the second thing?" Tanya asked. She crossed her arms in front of her chest and gave him a frosty glare.

"I don't want you to be upset, Tanya." His voice had softened, and his eyes were a little warmed. "But I'm worried that you're getting tangled up in our . . . whatever it is." He paused. "Our thing."

"I don't even know how to respond to what you just said." Tanya felt a cold wave of dread wash over her. She had hit on a calm, eerie place inside herself—a place that was prepared to say good-bye to Major forever.

He sighed. "You know my stance, Tanya." Why did he keep saying her name? Every time her name passed through those soft, full lips, she felt a corkscrew in the heart.

"Refresh my memory," she said. Not that she needed refreshing. It was his stance on commitment that had kept her awake so many nights, tossing and turning and praying that he would change his mind.

"I'm not looking for some complicated relationship. You and I have fun together . . . but I'm nowhere near ready for anything more than fun." He paused. "I don't know if I'll *ever* be ready."

"You don't seem to have a problem with having a relationship with Faith!" Tanya yelled. "She's *living* here."

"Tanya—"

"Is she or is she not staying in your apartment?" Tanya interrupted. *Please say no. Please. Please.*

"Yeah, she is staying here. But—"

"Don't. Just don't." Tanya had to leave. She had to put as much distance between herself and Major Johnson as the city of San Francisco would allow.

She was tempted to tell Major to drop dead or drive an ice pick through his skull. But Tanya did neither. Instead she took a deep breath, executed a graceful pivot, and let herself quietly out of the apartment.

Then she sprinted down the stairs as if she were being pursued by a wild dog. Or an angry grizzly bear. Or worse.

Thursday afternoon Blue lightly rubbed @café's malfunctioning cappuccino maker on its side. Through trial and error she had discovered that the machine responded well to a little TLC. The café was fairly crowded, and she had three cappuccino orders backed up already.

Thankfully all employees scheduled for duty had actually shown up for work. Even better, she and Jason seemed to have finally smoothed things over once and for all. They had eaten lunch together perched on the milk crates that littered the alley behind the coffeehouse. Jason hadn't mentioned Celia once . . . which was exactly what constituted a good conversation in Blue's mind.

"Let's see some foam, sister," she said to the

machine, giving it another pat. "I know the juices are flowing somewhere inside that hard metal exterior."

Behind Blue, someone (a he someone, from the sound of it) cleared their throat. Uh-oh. If this guy wanted a cappuccino, he was in for a long wait. Blue turned around, prepared to suggest to her new customer that he try a nice, refreshing iced coffee. "The machine's not—"

"Hey, Blue." Christian Sands grinned at her from the other side of the counter.

"Uh, hi!" Her overly bubbly voice sounded foreign to her.

"Are you all right?" Christian asked.

*No.* "Yes. Of course. I mean, why wouldn't I be all right?" *Aside from the fact that I sound like an idiot.*

"You look kind of pale," Christian answered. "And your hands are shaking."

Jeez! Her stupid hands—they betrayed her every time. "I didn't get a lot of sleep last night," Blue said. "And I've, uh, had a lot of coffee today. You know, the jitters."

Christian smiled. "Maybe you should stick to Sanka for a while."

"Can I, uh, get you anything?" Blue asked. Images were starting to flash before her eyes. The kiss she and Christian shared in his black Jeep, the *many* kisses they had shared in her fevered dream, the one kiss she had allowed herself to fantasize about for exactly twenty seconds last night before she had fallen asleep. She chose *not* to focus on the other fantasy she'd had—the one in which Jason had snuck into her room and kissed her lightly on the lips as if she were Sleeping Beauty (gag).

"I'd say that I'm not here for the coffee, but that's probably a line you hear about twenty times a day," Christian answered.

Blue tried to chuckle. She snorted instead. "Yeah, well, you know how it is."

She was surprised that he was here. They had gone out on a date, had a good time, and then briefly made out. At which point Blue totally freaked because she wasn't used to the disturbing sensations that were flowing through her as the kiss went on and on. When she had jumped out of the Jeep and sprinted into her house, Blue had assumed that Christian thought she was a freak and would never want to see her again. Now he was standing right in front of her. And he looked happy.

"So . . . what are you doing tonight?" Christian asked.

A dull roaring filled Blue's ears. Unless she had the IQ of a dodo bird, she was right to think that Christian had just asked her out for another date. Kind of. Okay, he was working *toward* asking her out for another date. "Uh . . ." *Good response. Way to go.*

The truth was that the mere idea of going on a second date terrified her. Blue had made a pact with herself to avoid all things romantic. She simply wasn't equipped to deal with the consequences of all that hearts and flowers stuff. She planned to live the life of a nun, minus all that annoying stuff about religion.

"Do you want to go to a movie?" Christian asked. "Or the beach? Or dinner?"

Jeez. With all of these options how could she say no? *Lie.* "Um, I've already got plans . . . unfortunately. I promised Jason that I would help him with his, uh, computer. It's got this weird virus thing, and he can't figure out why every time he opens a document, the whole thing comes out as, like, a zillion *x*s." *Babble, babble, babble. Drone, drone, drone.* She was truly pathetic.

Natalie suddenly appeared at Christian's side. "I thought Jason said he was going to Les Deux Gamines with Celia tonight."

Blue was aware of two facts simultaneously. (1) She had just been caught in an outright lie. (2) She was filled with rage because Jason had neglected to mention that he had a hot date with Navel Ring Girl. No wonder he had mumbled and stared at the ground when she had asked him if he wanted to rent a video with her.

"Did I hear someone say my name?" Jason materialized behind Natalie's shoulder. This mildly uncomfortable situation was rapidly turning into *Nightmare on Elm Street: Part Twenty-seven.*

"If you're Jason, then Natalie just said you

have a date with someone named Celia tonight," Christian said brightly, much to Blue's horror.

Jason glanced at Christian, then at Blue. Then back at Christian. "Yeah. So?"

"*So*, I was explaining that I was under the impression that you and I were going to do some, uh, computer work tonight." Blue was going down in flames, and she knew it.

Jason looked confused. Natalie looked as if she realized she had said the wrong thing. Christian looked blissfully unaware of what was going on around him.

"Hey, I've got a good idea," Christian said in the ensuing silence.

"What's that?" Natalie asked, although Blue still wasn't sure why Natalie was even involved in this conversation.

"How about a good old-fashioned double date?" Christian suggested. "You and Jason can even do some computer stuff before we all meet up."

"Uh . . ." Blue felt as if she had sucked the helium out of one very large balloon. "I don't think Jason would be too psyched for that. He's sort of . . . um . . ."

"Let's do it," Jason said suddenly. "A double date."

Christian grinned—Blue had never seen one guy grin so much during one five-minute conversation. Was it truly possible that there were people on this planet who were happy all the time? Okay, yes. The guy had an open, friendly, sincere, somewhat sexy smile. But still.

"Is that cool with you, Blue?" Christian asked.

"Huh," Blue said. She really couldn't imagine an entire evening of staring at Celia's various pierces. But at the moment she also couldn't imagine turning down Christian. "Sure."

"Great!" Christian responded. "I'll call you later to deal with logistics."

"Great," Jason echoed, with slightly less enthusiasm in his voice.

"Later," Blue said. Sure, her good-bye was a little abrupt. But she needed to get Christian out of the café and retreat to the safe haven of the women's room ASAP.

Christian waved and grinned yet again as he walked out of the café. He looked as good from the back as from the front—even a girl who was a confirmed nondater could appreciate that sort of detail. By the time Blue turned her attention back to Jason, Natalie had receded into the crowded café.

"So that's the guy," Jason commented.

Blue felt blood rush to her face. "Yep. I guess."

He nodded. "Tonight will be . . . interesting."

"Yeah, interesting," Blue echoed. She ran her now sweaty palms across the front of her apron and headed for the so-called powder room.

The prospect of a *Happy Days* style double date was nerve-racking at best, nightmarish at worst. Again Blue thought of the moment she and Jason had shared the other night. After days of zigzagging back and forth between arguing and stony silence, she and Jason seemed to have reached a concrete truce. When they had shaken hands on the deal, they had gotten closer and closer to each other . . . until at last their lips were just inches apart.

And then the moment had ended. Jason and Blue were best friends again, no strings attached. Now they were going on a double date . . . and Blue feared that those nonexistent strings would turn into a huge knot in the pit of her stomach.

For possibly the first time in her life Blue wondered what she should wear tonight. . . .

BACK    FORWARD    HOME    STOP

LINK: [                    ]

# DYLAN O'CONNOR: THE STATE OF @CAFÉ

First of all, let me say thanks to all of you who have been dropping by @café to sample our delicious coffee. When I first bought the café (throwing away all my college savings in the process), I was scared that the business wouldn't make it. Customers were put off by the fact that most of our computers kept crashing and our mugs were chipped and cracked.

But with hard work, traffic has picked up—recently we've even made a little money. Don't forget that I'm getting a kitchen installed. By the time school starts up again, all of you seniors who love to sneak off campus for lunch will be able to stop by @café for one of Natalie van Lenton's famous tuna avocado sandwiches (easy on the mayo for healthy living).

And as you know since you are reading this installment of Spill the Beans, all of us at @café toil weekly to bring you new material for your entertainment pleasure. But seeing only our stuff on the web site (no matter how witty and intelligent we may be) must get sort of old. So please, *please* submit your own items for publication. We'll post almost anything as long as there are no four-letter words or generally lewd language. If it sounds like I'm begging, I am. So please submit all entries to www.simonsays.com.

By the way, we *are* going to get the cappuccino maker fixed. Soon. I promise. In the meantime, how about a big mug of hot coffee?

"Sales were good today," Dylan said while closing Thursday night. "I think the business is finally getting solid." He was sitting at table six, totaling the day's receipts. The heat had rolled into San Francisco during the late afternoon, sending more customers into the café than in weeks.

"That's great!" Natalie called. She was at the sink, washing out a set of pink and blue coffee mugs. Even after an eight-hour shift her hair was shiny and her skin had a rosy glow.

"I've put aside enough extra cash for a new stove and a refrigerator," Dylan said. "I'm going to call a contractor next week to get an estimate on putting in the kitchen."

"Excellent," Natalie said. "Excellent."

Silence descended. Dylan searched his brain for another innocent comment about the doings of @café, but he couldn't think of anything else to say. How had this happened? It was 10:30 P.M., and he and Natalie were alone in the coffeehouse. This was not good. Not good at all.

"I'm going to the storeroom for a

**S
I
X**

second," Natalie called. "Do we need any napkins out here?"

Dylan scanned the café, checking the napkin dispensers. "I think we're fine, but go ahead and grab a couple of packages, anyway."

"Check." Natalie walked out from behind the counter and crossed the café to the door of the storeroom.

Dylan had tried not to study Natalie's figure as she walked by him, but it was impossible. In fact, he couldn't keep his eyes off her. She didn't move like a gazelle, exactly. Or like a cat. She moved more like a dolphin. If dolphins could walk, which of course they couldn't. So she moved like a—

"Dylan?" Natalie's voice broke through his very embarrassing thoughts. "Dylan, are you in there?"

He blinked. Natalie was standing at the door of the storeroom, holding up two different packages of napkins. "Sorry . . . I guess I was spacing out or something."

She smiled. "No problemo. I've found myself, uh, spacing out a couple of times today, too. Which napkins do you want to use? The old plain white ones?" She held up one package. "Or the new ones with the café logo?" She held up the other.

Dylan couldn't believe that they were lounging around discussing paper products. Who cared? He had Natalie all alone, and the only thing he could do was discuss receipts, coffee beans, and mopping techniques. Life sucked.

"Um, let's use the new ones," Dylan said. "We'll save the old for emergencies." Ah, the joy of making executive decisions.

She nodded and disappeared into the storeroom again. *Think about Sam,* Dylan ordered himself. *Think about your buddy and how he's going through the worst time in his life.* Dylan exhaled. Okay. All romantic thoughts about Natalie were now banished from his mind. He was free to resume normal, mundane life. Back to the adding machine.

Tap, tap, tap. Tap, tap, tap. Man, what was she *doing* in there? Dylan tapped his pencil against the table in a steady, droning rhythm. Maybe Natalie couldn't stand the sight of him. She was probably counting every stupid coffee bean in the storeroom just so she didn't have to look at his pathetic, miserable face. In fact, their kiss the other night had probably just been some hallucination brought on by sleep deprivation and desperation. Natalie actually *was* in love with Sam. . . . He closed his eyes and dropped his head onto the adding machine.

He felt Natalie sit down beside him. "This is tough," she said quietly. "Now I know why we decided we shouldn't be alone together."

Dylan nodded, but he didn't remove his head from the top of the adding machine. Looking into Natalie's eyes was simply too dangerous right now. "It won't happen again," he mumbled. "I'll make sure to schedule us on different shifts." Not that he hadn't already tried that.

He was going to have to have a serious talk with Blue. His little sister's annoying habit of skipping out on work whenever the mood struck was not something he was going to continue to tolerate. Not even if she pleaded and begged and threatened to tell their parents about the time Dylan took out Mr. O'Connor's car when he was fourteen.

"Oh!" Natalie said suddenly. "There's Sam."

Dylan sat up. If there was ever a time that three was a crowd, this was going to be it. And he was number three. Sam pushed open the door of the café and plopped into the La-Z-Boy.

"Hey, guys." Sam's voice was heavy with fatigue, but his smile was warm and friendly. "Man, I'm glad to see the two of you."

"How's it going, buddy?" Dylan asked, hoping he sounded both sincere and guilt-free.

Sam shrugged. "Well, I dropped my mom off at the rehab center," he said, running his fingers through his obviously unwashed hair. "It seemed all right . . . as far as those places go."

Natalie's face had softened. She seemed to be totally focused on Sam. As she should be. "Oh, Sam, that must have been terrible."

She slipped out of her chair and walked over to the La-Z-Boy. Sam held his arms wide open, at which point Natalie nestled into his lap. Dylan felt like barfing.

"So, is your mom dealing okay?" Dylan asked.

"Yeah." Sam wrapped his arms around Natalie's waist and hugged her close. "But I'm sure glad to see some friendly faces."

"How's Eddie?" Natalie asked. She ran her hand across Sam's cheek, causing a stabbing pain of jealousy to wend its way through Dylan's central nervous system.

"He's hanging in there," Sam said. "I stopped by the houseboat on my way here, and he was sound asleep."

Dylan had made it a policy to close up shop himself as many nights as possible. But this was too painful to bear. Natalie didn't look like a girl whose heart was breaking because she couldn't be with the one she loved. She looked like she was *with* the one she loved.

"Whoa, I can't believe this," Dylan started. "But I think I've got a mega-migraine coming on." That wasn't far from the truth. Since the second Natalie had made herself comfortable on Sam's lap, Dylan's temples had been throbbing painfully.

"Do you want some aspirin?" Natalie asked. She gave him a (possibly meaningful) look.

"Uh, no, thanks. I think I'd better get home and crash." Dylan switched off the adding machine and stood up. "Would you guys mind closing up?"

"Be happy to, my man," Sam said. "Anything for you."

"Thanks," Dylan said. "Night."

As Natalie and Sam called out their good-byes Dylan practically sprinted to the door. Within three seconds he was on the street, breathing in the warm night air. He paused outside the café. *Walk,* he ordered himself. *Don't look back.*

Slowly Dylan turned toward the large window at the front of @café. The street was fairly dark, so he was able to see inside all too easily. Again he couldn't stop himself as he looked closer.

Natalie and Sam were kissing. And this wasn't a peck-on-the-cheek-I'm-sorry-you-had-a-bad-day kiss. This was a full-on passionate kiss, complete with wandering hands. Dylan clutched his head.

Watching Sam and Natalie together wasn't just going to be hard. It was going to kill him.

"So I told the guy that if he wouldn't let me get my eyebrow pierced without a note from my parents, I would walk outside and forge a letter myself," Celia was saying. "And *he* said fine, but I had to get it notarized."

Blue dipped another french fry into the bowl of thin brown gravy and studied Celia. The girl *was* pretty, in sort of a I'm-so-hip-that-even-my-sheets-are-polyester kind of way. But her stories tended to go on forever.

"What happened?" Christian asked politely.

Blue, however, noticed that his jaw muscles were tensed. So far Christian and Celia had argued about religion, politics, and whether or not Diane or Rebecca was a better member of the gang at *Cheers.*

"I ended up getting someone else to do it," Celia said. "There's no shortage of people willing to pierce eyebrows in Frisco."

"So where's the eyebrow ring?" Blue asked.

Celia flicked her long dyed-red hair over one shoulder and bit into the pickle that had come with the grilled cheese she had ordered at Smiley's All Night Diner. "It got infected. I had to take it out because all this pus was oozing out and dripping into my eye—"

"There goes my appetite," Christian interrupted. He pushed away his half-eaten waffle sundae and made a gagging motion.

Blue glanced at Jason across the table. He winked (an actual wink) and grinned. "So, uh, how about those Forty Niners?" he asked no one in particular.

"I hear they're going to have a great season," Blue answered. "I think that one guy is going to hit, like, fifty home runs."

Christian laughed. "The Forty Niners are a football team, Blue."

"Oh." Well, she had tried.

So far this double date wasn't exactly what Mama had ordered from the apple pie shop. They had started the evening by strolling through a small art gallery that happened to be providing free cheese and crackers. Celia and Christian had embarked on a bitter debate about the relative merits of abstract art versus realist art, at which point Blue and Jason had retreated to a corner and talked about whether or not there was anything they could do to cheer up Sam.

The group had proceeded to the marina, where conversation had been so lagging that Blue had resorted to delivering a lecture about the first guy who ever crossed the Pacific Ocean in a one-man sailboat. And now they were here, and things didn't seem to be going all that much better.

But at least Blue wasn't suffering any from watching Jason and Celia together. On the scale of one to ten, her date was a definite eight. Celia barely ranked a three. If Jason wanted to waste his time with a girl who thought Boutros Boutros-Ghali was a small island in the South Pacific, then that was his problem.

"I'm getting pretty tired," Jason said during the ensuing lull in conversation. "I had to be at work early this morning."

"Yeah, maybe we should call it a night," Blue said quickly.

When four people were all equally intent on getting out of a place, it was amazing how quickly business could be transacted. In the space of one hundred and twenty seconds

Christian had signaled the waiter for their bill, Jason had announced the total, and four of them had dug into their pockets and pulled out six dollars each. With only minor shuffling of bags and various discarded outer shirts, they were out of the booth and at the door of the restaurant.

"Let's book," Blue said to Christian. "My dad will blow a gasket if I'm not home soon."

They walked quickly across the parking lot, leaving Jason and Celia dawdling next to a gum ball machine near the entrance of the diner. Blue climbed into Christian's Jeep and pulled the seat belt across her chest.

"That was a very, uh, different, sort of evening," Christian commented as he slid the key into the ignition. "I feel like I just spent three hours with Elvira's daughter."

Blue laughed. "There's no accounting for taste." In the rearview mirror she saw Jason and Celia making their way toward Celia's car. "Oops, here they come."

"Good night!" Celia screeched.

"Night," Jason echoed.

As Blue yelled out an appropriate good-bye Christian peeled out of the diner parking lot and turned onto Lopez Boulevard. Blue smiled to herself as Christian drove through the hilly streets that led to the O'Connors' home. Celia had played nice tonight—clearly the girl had come to realize how important Blue was to

Jason. Blue was even willing to bet that Celia regretted the fact that she had breezed into the café last week and told Blue to keep her hands off Jason. Good.

"Jason seems like a nice enough guy," Christian commented. "But he's clearly insane."

Blue turned to him. "Why is that?"

"How could he know a girl as awesome as you are and then turn around and date someone as lame as Celia?" Christian reached out and squeezed her hand. "The guy must be out of his mind."

Blue laughed. At this moment she felt deliciously normal. She was a normal girl, on a normal date, with a normal (cute) guy. Maybe she was going to get the hang of this adolescence stuff after all.

One thing was definite. Tonight Blue wasn't going to freak out and become a psycho when Christian kissed her good night. Nope. She planned to thoroughly enjoy every second of their inevitable lip lock. . . .

The key was in the same place it had always been. Jason didn't know why he was surprised—he had been to Blue's house a million times, and the key was always there.

Jason slid the key into the lock of the O'Connors' back door and turned it as slowly and quietly as possible. Tonight had been something of a disaster, but Jason felt strangely elated. He and Blue had charted new waters together—and they had come through relatively unscathed. Forget the fact that her dude was totally lame. At least they had managed to go out and no major conflicts had occurred.

After an hour of making out with Celia in her garage slash rec room, Jason had gone home and tried to go to sleep. He had really, really tried. In the past whenever he couldn't sleep, he had snuck out of his house and ridden his bike to Blue's. After an extended internal debate Jason had concluded that seeing as he and Blue were *still* best friends, he was *still* entitled to show up at her home unannounced.

The door groaned as Jason inched it open. This was a risky mission. Mrs. O'Connor was still awake—through the kitchen window Jason had seen her washing a sinkful of dishes. He was also fairly sure that Mr. O'Connor was roaming around the premises.

Every single step seemed to groan as Jason tiptoed carefully up the narrow stairway that led to Blue's third-floor bedroom. At the top of the stairs he tapped lightly on her closed door. No answer. *Three, two, one.* Jason pushed open the door and darted into the dark room.

He felt his way over to Blue's futon mattress and crouched next to her. "Blue!" he hissed. She was definitely there . . . and asleep. Even in the dark he could see the outline of her body beneath a thin cotton sheet. "Blue!"

Her eyes popped open. "Aaah!" she shrieked. Quickly Jason put his hand over her mouth. If Mr. and Mrs. O'Connor ran upstairs and found their little girl screaming, they were *not* going to be happy.

"It's me," he whispered. "Don't scream." Jason removed his hand and leaned back on his heels.

"Are you trying to give me a heart attack?" Blue hissed.

He wasn't. But his own heart felt perilously close to exploding. He wasn't prepared for the way that being so close to Blue in a dark room was making him feel. "Sorry. But I didn't want the parental units to discover their intruder."

Blue rubbed her eyes and wriggled into a sitting position. "What are you *doing* here?"

He shrugged. "I couldn't sleep."

"Why didn't you throw a rock at the window like you usually do?" she asked. She seemed to have recovered from her initial shock.

"I saw your mom downstairs," Jason explained. "I had to be extra sneaky."

"Oh." Blue grabbed a bottle of water that was sitting on the floor next to her mattress and took a long gulp. "Tonight was pretty much a disaster, huh?"

Jason nodded. "I don't think we'll be doing the foursome thing again anytime soon."

"It was fun being out with you, though,"

Blue said. "I mean, you and I haven't really hung out for a while."

Jason couldn't have agreed more. He had missed Blue—her laughter, her jokes, the mischievous gleam in her light blue eyes. "Do you really like that guy?" Jason asked. "I mean, is he going to be, like, your boyfriend?"

Blue was silent for a moment. "I don't know," she said finally.

Jason felt a pang of jealousy that nearly made him groan out loud. "You can do better," he said.

"That's *your* opinion," Blue said angrily. "Besides, you're in *no* position to comment on who anyone else chooses to date."

Jason sighed. Maybe coming over here to go through a blow-by-blow of the night's events hadn't been such a good idea. He didn't know exactly what he had hoped would happen when he arrived here, but this definitely *was not* it.

From now on he was going to cure his insomnia with sit-ups and push-ups.

Late night excursions to Blue's were about to become a thing of the past. And that made him sad. More sad than he cared to admit.

## SAM BARDIN OFFERS TIPS ON THIS SUBJECT:
### How to Make a Movie with Your Friends

First of all, once you endeavor to make a film (no matter how short) with a group of your friends, let me assure you that said friends will most likely not fall into that particular category by the time the making of the movie is complete. In my experience collective creative projects breed competition, frustration, general disillusionment, and egomania. Nonetheless, we all want (and <u>should</u> want) to express ourselves and the zeitgeist of our crowd. This being the case, I would like to offer some helpful hints as to how to avoid turning your best friend into your worst enemy through the making of <u>Bud</u> <u>Frenzy</u> <u>Goes</u> <u>to</u> <u>Algebra</u> <u>Class:</u> <u>A</u> <u>Love</u> <u>Story.</u>

1. This is important, so listen up. Once you and your buddies come up with the idea that you're sure is going to make you a million bucks in Hollywood, put that idea aside for a couple of days. Don't proceed with your project until you've reexamined the concept and decided that it really is genius and not just the product of several bored teenagers drinking way too much coffee during one long afternoon.

2. Make sure that just <u>one</u> of you is in charge of the actual filmmaking. If more than one person has the power to make decisions pertaining to the final scripts, various shots, and casting, all hell can break loose before you've even had the chance to see just what bad actors your friends really are.

3. Don't ignore tip #2 just because you're positive that you and your friends are so tight that nothing as trivial as petty bickering over close-ups versus long shots could tear you apart.

"You're right," Sam declared Friday morning. "Bob Ross is very soothing."

Natalie smiled. Finally she had found a convert. For years Natalie had watched Bob Ross's painting show on PBS—she found that his calm, hippie voice made her feel blanketed in a warm cocoon of love and security. When he died, she had cried and immediately started taping the reruns.

"I'm glad you're learning to appreciate the finer things in life," she said.

Sam tightened his arm around Natalie and dropped a kiss on the top of her head. They were sitting on the flowered sofa that filled most of the small den at the back of the Bardins' houseboat. On the coffee table in front of them sat a bowl of pretzels, a bag of Cool Ranch Doritos, and a large mushroom pizza.

Natalie snuggled closer to Sam. She felt a lot of warm fuzzies in his arms. Maybe this was where she was meant to be after all. With Dylan her emotions seemed to be wildly out of control. Sam made her

**SEVEN**

feel a steady stream of dependable affection. And Sam was the one who had made her feel beautiful long before Dylan looked at her as anything besides a little sister.

"I'm feeling a lot better, Nat," Sam said, giving her another squeeze.

"I'm glad," she responded. "You deserve to be happy, Sam. Never forget that."

He pulled away and looked straight into her eyes. "You're the reason for any happiness in my life right now. I hope you know that."

"You make me happy, too," Natalie said. And she meant it.

Being needed was a wonderful thing. Natalie had more or less lived to nurture since she was four years old. Looking out for her dad was one of her main missions in life, and she was always the person her friends turned to in time of need. Natalie knew herself well enough to realize that she thrived on *being there* for someone. And Sam was fulfilling that want . . . that need.

Of course, Dylan met her needs, too. But those were of a different sort. Those were the needs of a woman . . . not a girl. And maybe Natalie was happy to stay a girl a little longer. If finding out that her mother was still alive had taught her anything, it was that life threw plenty of complications in one's path as it was. There was no reason to go looking for more.

"What happened to Eddie?" Natalie asked.

"I hope we didn't make him feel like he was in our way."

"I'm in here!" Eddie yelled. "The kitchen."

"The boy has good ears," Natalie commented.

Sam rolled his eyes. "He was probably listening to every word we said."

"No, I wasn't," Eddie said, appearing at the door of the den. "Except for the part about how *happy* Natalie makes you." He pretended to gag. "Yuck!"

"Why don't you go do something?" Sam asked. "Nat and I need quality time by ourselves."

Eddie squeezed in next to Natalie on the sofa. "There's nothing *to* do," he moaned. "This houseboat is so *depressing*—I feel like we're living in a floating tomb."

Natalie felt a wave of sympathy for Eddie. He spent all his time either busing tables at the café or skulking around the house. Not much of a summer.

"You know what, Eddie?" Sam said suddenly. "You're right."

"Come on, guys," Natalie said quickly. "This place is great. And your mom will be home soon—"

"No, Eddie's right," Sam interrupted. "We're acting like *our* lives are totally messed up instead of our parents' lives."

"Why do I get the feeling that you're planning something?" Natalie asked.

He grinned. "Because I am." He paused dramatically. "As of today, the Bardin brothers are officially out of mourning. And we're going to have a party."

"A party?" Natalie echoed.

Eddie pumped his fist in the air in true fifteen-year-old-guy fashion. "All right!" he yelled. "Par-taaay!"

Images of broken lamps, beer-stained couches, and vomit-filled corners instantly popped into Natalie's head. "Are you sure a party is such a good idea?" she asked. "I mean, without any parental supervision things could get seriously out of hand—"

"My mind is made up," Sam said. "I'm having a party." He jumped off the couch and started to pace across the small room. "And this isn't going to be some lame get-together where we hang out and play poker. I'm going to have an all-out bash."

Natalie still wasn't sure that a big party at the houseboat was the hottest idea—but since Sam was determined, there was no point in being nonsupportive. "I'll make some french onion dip," she offered. "And maybe some fried calamari and asparagus rolls . . ."

Sam was still pacing. He clapped. *"Finally* I have something to think about besides the fact that my dad is in jail and my mom is in rehab. It's time to get my main man Dylan out of his love funk."

"Can I invite some of my friends?" Eddie asked.

"Sure," Sam answered. "Why not?"

Maybe this party was a good idea after all. Eddie had been living in virtual isolation since Mr. Bardin had gone away—it was possible that showing off for his pals in front of his older brother's friends would give him a boost.

"Yes!" Eddie shouted.

"What were you saying about Dylan?" Natalie asked. *Casual. Stay casual.* It was perfectly normal for her and Sam to talk about Dylan. After all, they both considered him one of their closest friends.

Sam plopped back down on the couch. "Dylan and Tanya broke up over a year ago, right?"

"Right." Natalie sensed they were getting into dangerous territory. Her breathing was now slightly labored.

"Since Dylan broke up with Tanya, how many girls has he dated?"

"Uh, none." Which was technically true. Dylan and Natalie had certainly never *dated.*

"Which means the guy hasn't even *kissed* a girl since then." A pained expression crossed Sam's face.

"Uh-huh." Okay, now she was lying. This was an outright, bold-faced lie. And Natalie had a sinking feeling that as of this moment, the lies were going to be piling up one after another.

"I'm going to invite so many cute girls to my party that Dylan won't be able to help himself from asking at least one of them out on a date."

Natalie dug her fingers into the couch. There was only one interpretation of Sam's statement. Sam wanted to set Dylan up on a date. He wanted Dylan to find a nice pretty girl who he could make out with on moonlit nights under the stars. And that girl certainly wasn't going to be Natalie.

"Uh, maybe Dylan doesn't *want* to date," she pointed out. "I mean, he's so busy with the café that he barely has time to sleep." *Lies, lies, lies.*

Sam rolled his eyes. "Nat, you're so sweet."

Hmmm. This wasn't the response she had expected . . . or even the one she had hoped for. *You're absolutely right. Dylan can find his own girl.* That had been the response she had wanted. As for what she had *expected* . . . she wasn't sure.

"What do you mean, 'sweet'?" she asked.

Sam laughed. "No matter what else a guy has to deal with in his life, he's *always* interested in the opposite sex. Always."

"Oh." Well, Sam was the authority.

"Trust me, the reason Dylan is always so uptight and grouchy is that he doesn't have a nice girl like you to wrap his arms around during Bob Ross reruns."

Was that an ulcer forming in her stomach? The idea of Dylan with his arms wrapped around anyone besides her was intolerable. "Um, so . . . what are you saying?"

"I'm going to find Dylan the girl of his dreams—this Saturday night." Sam was beaming, and his voice was filled with more energy than Natalie had heard in it since before Mrs. Bardin had gone into the hospital.

She was glad for Sam—but crushed for herself.

For once Jason was actually grateful that he had a shrink. For almost two years Jason had been wheedled into making the trek to Dr. Grady's office every week. Jason usually spent the fifty-minute sessions sitting sullenly in one of the psychiatrist's comfortable chairs. He spoke as little as possible.

"I'm sorry I had to change our appointment to today," Dr. Grady said as soon as Jason sat down. "I had some family business to attend to."

Interesting. Shrinks took some kind of vow not to say anything about their personal lives to patients. For the first time it struck Jason that Dr. Grady even had a family. "No problem," Jason said. "Today worked out better for me, anyway."

Dr. Grady pushed his tortoiseshell-rimmed glasses up on his nose and leaned back in his chair. This was his time-to-get-down-to-business pose. "So . . . tell me what's going on."

Jason took the kind of deep, cleansing breath that Blue had taught him how to do last year when Jason kept insisting he was going to kick the crap out of their biology teacher, Mr. Boyd. He wasn't used to the concept of having a concrete topic to discuss with Dr. Grady. This took some getting into.

"I have something to say." Okay, that was as much as he could get out in one breath.

"Wonderful!" Dr. Grady said. Jason could tell that the shrink was trying to hide his shock. "Have you been thinking about the incident?"

Ugh. Dr. Feel-good couldn't go one session without mentioning that night. The night that drove Jason over the edge and into the loony bin. Thank goodness Dr. Grady had a no-pressing policy. "No," Jason said. "This is about Blue . . . you know, Blue?"

"Of course," Dr. Grady said, making some kind of notation on the yellow pad sitting in his lap. "Blue is the girl you think of as your best friend."

"I don't just *think* of her as my best friend. She *is* my best friend." Jason hated the way Dr. Grady put everything into terms of thoughts and feelings. Some things just *were*.

"Yes, yes. Of course." He laced his fingers together and gave Jason one of his quizzical looks.

"I'm, uh . . ." How to go on? How to reveal The Secret?

"Yes . . ." Dr. Grady's voice was encouraging.

"I'm in love with her." Was that his breath leaving his lungs faster than the speed of light? Jason immediately had the sense that his brain had exploded.

He hadn't slept last night. After he had stumbled out of Blue's room, he rode his bike around town for hours. Near dawn Jason found himself at the beach.

*Jason let his bicycle fall to the sand. The first rays of sunlight were shining across the Pacific Ocean, making the dark, churning water sparkle as if it were dusted with tiny diamonds. He had always come to the beach for two reasons. The first was joy and the second was sadness. This morning Jason wasn't sure why he had found himself at the shore.*

*He kicked off his black Converse low tops and dug his toes deep into the sand. The grains felt wet and cold against his skin, and a cool breeze ruffled the hair at the nape of his neck. Jason walked to the edge of the water and sank onto the white sand. Small waves lapped his ankles as he stared out at the horizon.*

*A single thought had been kicking around in his brain since last night. He had hoped that if he surfed the web for enough hours or rode his bike far enough, the thought would dissolve. But as the hours passed he had become more and more restless . . . more consumed by The Thought.*

*Now Jason breathed in the fresh morning air and allowed The Thought to take shape within his consciousness. It had started over a year ago, when he had met Blue in detention. The connection had been instant . . . and Jason's whole life had changed. Blue had made him feel like a part of the world again. She had validated him in a way that loosed the ties that had bound his soul. She had made him free. Free to care, free to be himself, free to laugh. And now . . . and now Jason realized that she had made him free to love.*

*"I am in love with Blue," he whispered to the sea. "I'm in love with her, and—"*

"I want to do something about it," Jason finished the thought for Dr. Grady.

The psychiatrist grinned—a first. "Wonderful!" he exclaimed.

Jason felt a little like a kindergartner who had just been praised by his teacher for managing to draw within the lines of a coloring book picture, but at the moment he didn't mind Dr. Grady's slightly patronizing manner. He was just relieved to have outside approval for the somewhat crazy ideas that had been swirling in his head for weeks.

"So, uh, I guess I need to figure out what exactly I'm going to do," Jason said hesitantly.

Dr. Grady nodded. "Have you considered telling Blue how you feel?"

Jason's mouth suddenly felt like it was filled

with a very large cotton ball. "Uh, I've *considered* telling her . . . but I don't know if it's something I could really go through with."

"Hmmm . . ." Dr. Grady nodded as if he were mulling over a calculus equation.

"Right?" Jason prompted. "I mean, I can't say something like . . . well, like the thing I said and then just do *nothing.*" He paused. "Can I?"

Dr. Grady didn't seem prepared to help him out. The shrink kept nodding and looking wise, but he said nothing. "Hmmm . . ." Okay, *almost* nothing.

"*Talk* to me," Jason begged. "I need *help.*" Had anyone ever told Jason that he would one day be pleading with Dr. Grady for concrete advice, Jason would have promptly shoved the person's head in a toilet and flushed several times.

Dr. Grady crossed one knee over the other and nodded yet one more time. "What's the worst thing that will happen if you reveal your feelings to Blue?" he asked.

Jason felt a layer of sweat form at his hairline. "Lightning will strike me down?" he suggested tentatively.

Dr. Grady was *not* amused. "Seriously, Jason. Consider the question seriously."

More sweat. It was dripping down his face now. "Um . . . she'll tell me that I'm a totally disgusting individual who doesn't deserve to be on the same planet with her?"

The shrink shrugged. "Okay, let's say Blue *does* say that."

"Uh-huh . . ." Jason didn't like the road on which this rap session was traveling. What happened to the encouraging words of support he had come to expect from the doctor?

*"Now,* what is the *best* thing that could happen?" He looked at Jason expectantly.

Major mental meltdown time. Jason was more or less convinced that an extremely strong, unpleasant odor was working its way from his armpits to the general atmosphere of the office. "She'll tell me she loves me back," Jason said quietly. Even saying the words out loud made him feel like he was living out a dream.

"Good," Dr. Grady said in his most approving, enthusiastic voice. "Blue returning those feelings is the best thing that could come as a result of you expressing yourself."

"But there's, like, no way that Blue is going to tell me she loves me. I mean, she doesn't even believe in dating." Of course, Blue *was* basically going out with a guy right now. Which was a whole other issue.

"Whether or not you say something to Blue is entirely your decision," Dr. Grady said. "But I will tell you that I believe learning to express yourself freely is an important step for you . . . no matter what the outcome."

Jason loathed to admit that his shrink might have a valuable point buried in his psychobabble.

But when a guy made sense, he made sense. "I guess I would feel sort of . . . free . . . if I just let it all hang out." There was that word again. *Free.*

"I think we're getting somewhere, Jason." Dr. Grady looked like he had just discovered the first gold mine in California. "You're making a very important connection to your being . . . your essence."

Jason wanted to be cynical. He wanted to be jaded. But his heart was pounding, and his blood was rushing. "I'm going to do it," he declared. "I'm going to tell Blue how I feel."

The weight of the world was suddenly lifted from his shoulders. He had known that he was going to have to do *something*. Now he knew what that something was. Jason was going to be totally and brutally honest with the girl he loved.

And if the worst happened . . . then it happened. Either way Jason would be rid of the weight that had been around his neck for what felt like forever. As Dr. Grady glanced at his watch Jason stood up, feeling stronger and more powerful than he had since he was ten years old and learned to ride his bike no handed.

As of today Jason Kirk was a man of action. For better or for worse.

Dear Delia,

I can't call you Mom yet. Maybe I won't ever be able to . . . I don't know. But I've thought a lot about you since we met in Portland. I can't say that I understand what you did. I don't think anything would make me give up my husband and children the way you did. But things were different back then— maybe you were a product of the chaos brought on by the free love generation. I don't know.

A lot has been happening in my life this summer. It's been one of the times when I most wish I had a real "mom" to confide in. I have hopes and fears and dilemmas that are too much for a seventeen-year-old girl to handle without the guidance of someone older and wiser. Maybe if I had learned the truth about you earlier, we would know each other well enough by now that I would be able to talk to you about all of this stuff. As it is, you're still a stranger to me.

But you're a stranger who happens to be my mother. I want to get to know you—over time. I'd like to trade letters or e-mail with you and maybe even talk on the phone sometimes. Eventually I would like to see you again . . . if you want to see me, that is.

Let me know what you think about the things I've said. I'm very confused right now, and I'm willing to listen to any and all opinions regarding this situation. (Sorry if that sounded too formal.) Anyway, I hope everything is going well for you. I'd be more specific, but seeing as I don't know the first thing about your life, that's not possible.

Your daughter,

Natalie

Dylan set down the glass of iced tea he had been sipping from and glanced around the main dining room of Carl's Movie Café. Life-size glossy posters of stars lined the walls of the restaurant, and the jukebox in the corner played only songs from movie sound tracks. Basically every available inch of space was crammed with some movie-related piece of junk—a pair of Denzel Washington's suspenders, a motorcycle helmet that had supposedly belonged to James Dean, a Sharon Stone action figure. The place was cheesy with a capital C, but there was no question that business was booming.

"What are you going to have?" Dylan asked Tanya over the blare of the opening bars of the *Star Wars* theme song.

Tanya pursed her lips and studied the menu. "Either a Madonna Madness melon plate or the Kevin Costner chili burger deluxe." She glanced at him. "You?"

Dylan was truly regretting his

**EIGHT**

restaurant selection. "Um, I think I'll go with the Terminator tortilla platter."

Tanya set down her menu. She leaned forward and rested her bare elbows on the neon green surface of the table. "Why are we here?" she asked.

Dylan shrugged. "I told you—I wanted to see how these guys pack in so many willing victims." He scanned the restaurant again. "Once I get the kitchen installed, I'm going to have to think about how to get people to come to @café to eat."

"I certainly hope you're not planning to fill the café with crap like this," Tanya said, wrinkling her nose at a stiletto heel (something like the ones Uma Thurman had worn in *Pulp Fiction*) that was hanging on the wall over Dylan's head.

"No way," Dylan assured her. "This place is giving me a serious headache." He didn't add that his head had been pounding consistently since he'd watched Natalie and Sam making out.

"Anyway, I wasn't asking why we're *here*." Tanya gave him a pointed look. "I was asking why you wanted to go out to dinner with me in the first place."

"Oh, that." There were advantages and disadvantages to remaining close to one's ex-girlfriend. One of the disadvantages was that Tanya knew Dylan well enough to cut through the bull and hone in on what was going on inside his head.

"Let me guess. You need to unburden your-self regarding the subject of Ms. Natalie van Lenton." Tanya tapped her manicured finger-nails against her glass of diet Coke and waited for an answer.

"I'm miserable," Dylan admitted. "I feel like I'm on the brink of total insanity."

Tanya sighed deeply. "Unfortunately I know *exactly* how you feel."

Man, he was a self-centered pig. He should have seen that Tanya wasn't her usual exuber-ant self. "More problems with Major?" he guessed.

Tanya rolled her eyes. "A *problem* is when a guy doesn't call back for a week. A *problem* is when the guy you're in love with fails to no-tice that you got a new haircut. I'm facing a relationship apocalypse."

"Uh, do you want to talk about it?" Dylan asked.

He almost felt like laughing. When he had walked in on Tanya cheating on him with that jerk Matthew Chance last summer, he never would have predicted that thirteen months later they would be consoling each other about their love lives. Yet here they were.

Tanya shook her head. "Talking about Major will only highlight the humiliation that defines my life. I'd rather talk about *you* and your particular brand of patheticness."

"Natalie told me that she cares about me . . .

really cares about me. But she can't break up with Sam because she feels it's important that she stand by him right now." He paused—a painful pause. "And I agree with her . . . one hundred percent." *Okay, maybe ninety-five percent,* he added silently.

Tanya's eyes widened. "Wow—she really told you that?"

Dylan nodded. "She wrote me a note and we met . . . and, well, you know. . . ."

She shook her head. "I *don't* know."

Dylan had thought that rehashing the story would make him feel as if he had released the steel band wrapped around his head. Nothing was further from the truth. "I thought girls told each other everything."

"So did I," Tanya agreed. "Apparently Natalie is good at keeping her mouth shut. Which is more than I can say for either of us."

"Well, no matter who tells who what, the basic facts are the same." Dylan pushed his iced tea away from his side of the table and grabbed a large plastic saltshaker. He felt the need to squeeze. "I'm doomed."

"I'm really sorry, Dylan," Tanya said quietly. "But I think you're giving up hope with Natalie too quickly."

He let go of the saltshaker. "You do?"

She nodded. "Natalie is a calm, rational, loyal person."

"Yeah, so?" Dylan failed to see how any of those qualities were going to work in his favor right now.

"I'm not finished," Tanya explained. "But underneath her Martha Stewart veneer she's also incredibly passionate."

"True." He had witnessed that passion firsthand. And it was extraordinary.

"She won't ignore her heart forever," Tanya said firmly. "And eventually you'll *both* realize that you're not doing Sam any favors by staying away from each other. He deserves someone who wants to be with him for the right reasons."

For the first time in days Dylan felt as if he could breathe. Maybe Tanya was right. He had never really looked at the situation from Sam's point of view. Of course a guy like Sam wouldn't want a mercy girlfriend. That wasn't his style. And even though it wasn't Dylan's place to convince Natalie that she was possibly making a mistake, he could at least hang on to the hope that she would eventually reach the same conclusion on her own. Or with the help of her best friend, Tanya.

Dylan managed a weak smile. "You're a lifesaver, you know that?"

"I try," she answered.

"What do you say we skip the Madonna melon plate and the Costner burger?" Dylan suggested. "This place is sucking the IQ right out of me."

Tanya pushed back her chair. "The sooner we escape, the better."

Dylan pulled a five-dollar bill out of his pocket and put it on the table. "How about we go to my place for grilled cheese sandwiches and tomato soup?"

"Cheap comfort food," Tanya commented. "I love it."

They walked through the crowded restaurant and out into the night. About twenty people were actually standing in line to get inside the place. "Don't go in there," Dylan warned. "By the time you come out, you'll have morphed into Marion Ross from *Happy Days*."

Suddenly Dylan felt an iron grip around his elbow. "What the—"

"Kiss me!" Tanya hissed. She spun Dylan around so that he was facing her.

"Excuse me?" This night was getting downright bizarre.

"Kiss me," she repeated. "Just *do* it."

"Tanya, I really don't think that's such a good—" He stopped midsentence as Tanya used her free hand to grab his neck and pull his head toward hers.

A split second later Dylan found himself in a serious lip lock with the girl who had just listened to him spill his guts. At least her lips were soft and full. And familiar. Seeing as he was stuck in the steel trap of Tanya's arms, Dylan decided that for once he would go with the flow. He relaxed his mouth and then moved his lips over hers again and again. Actually this wasn't such a bad remedy for what ailed him. Natalie was probably busy smooching Sam. Why *shouldn't* Dylan seek a little comfort in the arms of a loved one?

As unexpectedly as the kiss had begun, it ended. Tanya dropped her arms and pried herself away. "Thanks, Dylan."

She took a couple of steps away and started walking down the block. Dylan blinked rapidly. Was it possible that he was suffering from some kind of illness that made him experience periodic hallucinations? Maybe Tanya hadn't really kissed him. For that matter, maybe he had imagined everything that had gone on between him and Natalie. Perhaps it had been so long since his lips had made contact with another human being that he was starting to go insane.

Dylan jogged past the people waiting in line. Now that he was beside Tanya, he saw that her jaw was set and her dark eyes were filled with tears. Clearly something had happened. He clasped her arm and dragged her to a stop. "Do you want to tell me what that was about?"

She looked away. "No."

"Why don't you tell me, anyway." He wasn't going to take no for an answer.

"Most guys would love to be accosted by a beautiful girl on the street," Tanya snapped. "Why don't you just count the few blessings that come your way?"

"Give it up, T." He raised one arm and looped it around her shoulders. "Something is going on here."

Tanya's eyes were focused on some indistinguishable spot far down the street. "Major just walked by," she said tearfully. "With Faith."

Dylan was beginning to see the painful picture. "Who's Faith?" he asked gently.

"Major's girlfriend." The words were little more than a whisper, but Dylan heard them. He pulled Tanya closer and hugged her tightly.

"I'm sorry." What more could he say?

She pressed her face against his denim shirt and sobbed. "Am I ever going to stop feeling so horrible?" she asked.

He moved his hand up and patted her mass of curly hair. "You'll feel better someday," he assured her. "We both will."

Dylan kept his arms around Tanya and rocked her back and forth. He had heard that misery loved company, but at the moment he wished more than anything that at least one of them didn't feel like bursting into tears. If Tanya was right that grilled cheese sandwiches constituted comfort food, then he was going to be cooking all night. Because they both needed more comfort than one bear hug could provide. What they needed were some miracles.

Sam shifted uncomfortably on the stone bench he had been perched atop for the last fifteen minutes. The Hillbrook Rehabilitation Center had promised to provide a peaceful setting for his mother's "recovery." The place was so peaceful that Sam felt ready to jump out of his skin.

Mrs. Bardin paced back and forth in front of Sam and Eddie, who looked as uncomfortable as Sam felt. "I want you boys to know that you were absolutely right to send me here," she said for the fifth time. "I've only been here a little over twenty-four hours, and I already feel stronger than I have in months."

"That's great, Mom," Eddie said. "And don't worry, we'll come visit you every day."

Mrs. Bardin stopped pacing. "Well, that's one of the things I wanted to talk to you about tonight. I won't be allowed to have any phone calls or see any visitors for a week."

"Oh." Sam felt guilty over the relief that flooded through him. He loved his mother, but he couldn't say he relished the thought of driving out here once a day to watch her recovery.

"The counselors and therapists here have explained that I need to focus on just me for a while," Mrs. Bardin continued. "That way I'll get better faster."

"Okay," Eddie said quietly. He didn't look relieved. He looked heartbroken.

"But I've decided that as soon as I get out of here, we're all going to attend some family counseling." Mrs. Bardin looked at each of her sons in turn. "Do either of you object to that?"

Sam rolled his eyes. "How are we going to go to a family shrink when one of the members of our family is locked up in prison?"

Mrs. Bardin sank down beside him on the small bench. "We've all got to come to terms with our situation. And I think getting the subject out in the open and discussing our feelings about your father is going to be an important step in the process."

Oh, no. She was already sounding like a walking, talking self-help book. "Uh, sure, Mom. Whatever."

Far be it from Sam to stand in the way of putting their dysfunctional family on the road to repair. At their current rate of self-destruction, they were all headed straight for the *Montel Williams Show*. He could see the Montel segment in his mind.

*"Ladies and gentlemen, please welcome Margaret Bardin to the show." There's a light smattering of applause and a few snickers. "Margaret overdosed on alcohol and painkillers two months ago. She's joined on the stage by her two sons, Sam and Eddie. Via satellite we'll be talking to Margaret's husband, Joseph." Montel pauses.*

*Flash to a shot of Mr. Bardin, complete with a light blue jailhouse jumpsuit. "Joseph is currently in prison for fraud, income tax evasion, and extortion."*

*The audience gasps. This motley crew of a family is even more pathetic than the usual daily talk show fare. Everyone is excited to hear just where the whole thing went wrong. . . .*

"I'm glad I have your support, Sam." Mrs. Bardin reached up and ran her hand gently over the top of his head, the way she had when he was a little kid. "It means everything to me." She turned to Eddie. "How about you, hon?"

He nodded. "I'll do whatever you want, Mom."

Mrs. Bardin leaned across Sam and grasped her younger son's hand. "I knew I could count on you."

101

For several seconds the three of them sat on the bench in silence. Sam wondered if this was how adult children felt when they came to visit a parent at a nursing home. No matter how nice this place was, he still hated the idea of leaving his mother here all alone.

Mrs. Bardin glanced at the slim Cartier watch she still wore around her wrist. "I better get moving, kids. I have a group session in ten minutes."

Sam stood up. This visit hadn't been as traumatic as the one he had taken to visit his father in prison, but it wasn't exactly an evening he would remember fondly. "We need to get going, anyway," he said. "Eddie has a shift busing tables at the café tonight."

Mrs. Bardin stood, then hugged each of her sons. "I'm glad you boys are keeping busy."

"We're fine," Eddie said.

"He's right," Sam added. "We're doing fine."

Mrs. Bardin put one hand on each of Sam's shoulders and looked into his eyes. "I'm trusting you to take care of things for me, Sam. I know it's a big job, but we don't have anyone else to take charge right now."

"I know, Mom." He knew all too well. It was something he couldn't even begin to forget.

As he said good-bye, Sam decided against informing his mother about the party he was going to have tomorrow night. He had a feeling that she wouldn't approve of the idea of a hundred or more teenagers tearing through the houseboat. But nothing was going to keep him from throwing the biggest rager San Francisco had ever seen.

Besides, what was the worst thing that could happen?

# Yo, Yo, Yo
# I'm Talkin' to You!

Despair no more!

There is life after the Fourth of July.

Sam Bardin is inviting you

into his house and home.

That's right, people.

We're talkin' about a party!

Saturday night.

Dock #13, Pier Lane.

Please bring your own beverages.

"You make me feeel, you maaake me feeel, you make me feel like a natural *woman*," Blue sang Saturday morning as she walked around the café filling paper napkin dispensers.

"I neverrrr knewww what was wrong with meee *until* your kisss helped me naame *it*. Now I'm no longer doubtfullll of what I'm livin' fooor. . . ." Her voice trailed off as she noticed Natalie standing in the doorway of the café.

"Did Aretha Franklin die and reincarnate herself in your body or what?" she asked. Wearing black denim overalls and a light pink shirt at seven o'clock in the morning, Natalie looked as much like an Ivory girl as Blue did at a decent hour of the day.

"I'm happy," Blue said. "So I'm singing." She stepped over to table four and shoved a healthy supply of fresh napkins into the dispenser. "And for the record, Aretha Franklin is still alive and well doing shows at Radio City Music Hall."

Natalie lobbed her brown leather backpack over the counter and headed for the mug of coffee that Blue had poured herself as soon as she had got the urn going a few minutes ago. "Can I drown myself in this?" Natalie asked. "I'm feeling the need for a caffeine overhaul."

Blue noticed that despite her well put together outfit, Natalie looked tired. No, more like exhausted. "Help yourself," Blue said. My, she was feeling generous this morning. "There's plenty more where that came from."

Natalie picked up the mug and walked over to the cash register. She pushed a few buttons, and the drawer popped open. "What's got you so elated this morning?"

Blue shoved her last napkin into a nearly full dispenser. Natalie probably had no idea of the scope of the question she had just asked. Answering her could take the rest of the morning. "Let's just say I had a revelation."

Natalie wiggled her dark eyebrows. "A revelation? That sounds promising." She slammed the drawer shut again. "We need singles—and please, expand upon said revelation."

Late last night Blue had been sitting alone in the living room, watching a *Little House on the Prairie* rerun on some cable station that constantly replayed old hits such as *Eight Is Enough* and *Family Affair*. As always, Blue had been completely sucked into the world of Ma, Pa, Laura, Mary, and Carrie Ingalls. The perfect family, living on the perfect prairie, handling every life crisis in the most perfect way.

The episode's central story line had involved Almanzo (aka Manly) at last realizing that he was in love with Laura. Blue didn't like to think of herself as a person overly influenced by painfully sentimental television shows, but even she had moments of weakness. And watching Manly gaze into Laura's eyes with the dark prairie sky providing a vast, seamless background, Blue experienced one of those moments. Her blood didn't curdle at the thought of long walks in the moonlight, Saturday night square dances, or holding hands at church. Instead Blue felt a keen sense of yearning as she studied Melissa Gilbert's blissed-out face.

"I've decided that the whole boyfriend-girlfriend thing has some merit after all." Blue slid past Natalie and opened the door of the minirefrigerator behind the counter. She pulled out one carton of half-and-half and one carton of skim milk.

"Wow!" Natalie exclaimed. "What changed?"

Blue was silent for a moment. She had lain awake in bed last night asking herself the same question. "I don't know," she finally said. "Maybe I'm just ready to grow up . . . or something." She picked up the cartons and carried them to a small table next to the door of the café.

"Does this *revelation* have anything to do with your newfound feelings for Jason?" Natalie asked.

"Nope," Blue answered quickly. She had been prepared for that particular inquiry. In fact, she had wondered herself if her yen for the love of Almanzo had something to do with the way the actor's bright blue eyes resembled Jason's.

Blue set down the milk cartons and began to straighten various stacks of plastic lids. "Jason and I are friends. Period. And that's all we're ever going to be." Blue wasn't sure whether she was trying to convince herself or Natalie on that point, but she plowed ahead, anyway. "Christian, on the other hand, is a guy I could fall in love with." There. She had said it.

"Really?" Natalie frowned. "How do you know?"

Blue crossed her arms over the front of her gray Girls Kick Butt T-shirt. "What do you mean, how do I *know?*" What was there to know? Christian was nice, cute, and he liked her. Add to that the fact that he didn't make her want to throw up when he kissed her, and Blue felt he was the perfect male.

"You've only been out with the guy a few times," Natalie said. "You two don't really *know* each other."

"So what are you saying?" Blue asked. "I can't believe that after months of nagging me about my lack of a love life, you're going to try and persuade me not to go out with Christian."

Natalie raised her eyebrows. "I'm not trying to do anything. . . . I'm simply suggesting that you shouldn't leap into things. Take things slow."

Blue snorted. "If I go much slower, I'm going to be eighty-one by the time I get past kissing on the front doorstep of my house."

Natalie laughed. "Just don't get yourself in so deep with Christian that you can't get out of the relationship easily—just in case you realize he's not really the guy who's meant for you."

Blue sensed that there was some kind of subtext to what Natalie was saying, but it was far too early in the morning (even if she was feeling uncharacteristically perky) to embark on such a deep discussion. Instead Blue pointed to the yellow flyer Sam had tacked in the center of one of @café's large bulletin boards. "In your humble opinion, would I be moving too fast if I asked Christian to Sam's party tonight?"

Natalie laughed again. "I think that would be entirely appropriate." She picked up the mug and took another sip of coffee. "That party is really going to be something."

Blue headed for the phone. "Okay, here I go." Already her palms were sweating and her heart felt like a butterfly trying to break out of a tightly wrapped cocoon.

"You're calling him *now?*" Natalie shrieked. "It's not even nine o'clock yet."

Blue punched in the first three digits of Christian's phone number (which she had memorized at midnight the night before in an effort to focus all her energy on a specific, easily attained goal). "He's awake," Blue said confidently. "Christian goes surfing every morning at dawn." Blue dialed the last four digits. "You see, I know him better than you think."

"Hey, you go, girl," Natalie said. "I'll just sit back and watch the love story unfold."

The phone was ringing. Briefly Blue allowed herself to consider hanging up before anyone answered. But no, that wasn't an option. She had made an oath to herself last night that she was going to move forward into womanhood, and this was a first essential step.

"Hello?" Christian's voice was alert and cheerful. Blue immediately felt her heart rate even out to a steady two hundred or so beats per minute.

"Hey, Christian." Her voice sounded slightly breathy . . . maybe even a teeny, itsy, bitsy bit sexy.

"Blue!" Again enthusiasm. Her confidence level was rising by the millisecond. "This is a nice surprise."

Now what? Blue glanced at Natalie hopelessly. *"Ask* him," Natalie whispered. "Do it!"

"Yeah, well, you know. . . ." Now she knew how guys felt when they called up a girl to ask her out on a date. This was far from a pretty business.

"Know what?" Christian asked. Ah, so he was playing stupid. He probably wanted to get her back for the way she had hemmed and hawed and done everything but say a nice, definitive yes each time he had asked her out.

"Um, do you want to go to Sam Bardin's party with me tonight?" Blue asked. This was big. Sara Jane O'Connor had just asked a guy out on a date—voluntarily.

"Hey, are you asking me out?" Christian sounded as flabbergasted as she felt.

"I don't know if I'd call it a *date*," Blue said. "I mean, it will be night, and you and I will be together, and we may even dance or something . . . but I don't know if it's a date per se."

"I'd love to go—on one condition." He sounded happy, definitely happy.

"Uh, what's that?" Blue pictured herself in a black leather miniskirt, whip in hand. Conditions spelled peril.

"You have to answer one question." On the other end of the line Blue detected laughter. Or something.

"Sure, no problem." Answering a stupid question was easy. Six times six was thirty-six. The capital of Missouri was Jefferson City. De Nile wasn't just a river in Egypt. Sure, she could answer a question.

"Does the fact that you're asking me out on a date—or whatever you want to call it— mean that you actually like me?" The question just sort of hung there like a comma in the middle of a blank piece of paper.

*Say it!* Blue commanded herself. He wanted to hear that she liked him, and she *did* like him. Nothing, absolutely nothing was standing in the way. "Yes, I *like* you." Blue giggled—something she had never expected to find herself doing during a telephone conversation with a guy. Ever. But what the heck. "I like you!"

Freedom! Liberation! She had made use of the First Amendment. Blue had told a guy that she liked him. Whatever "like" meant.

"I'll pick you up at eight tonight," Christian said.

"Okay, great." It was that simple.

"Blue?" He was speaking more softly now.

"Yeah?" Her heart was still hammering. This was stupid—but somehow wonderful.

"Thanks for calling so early . . . and saying what you said." He paused. "You made my day."

"*De nada,* hombre," Blue answered. "I'll

see you tonight." She hung up the phone slowly, then turned to face Natalie.

"Well?" Natalie looked encouraging—sort of like a new mother who was waiting for her child to crawl for the first time.

"Christian and I are going to Sam's party together," Blue announced. "We're on our way."

Natalie held out her hand for a high five. "All right!" she yelled. "I hope everything goes how you want it to."

Blue slapped Natalie's hand. She shared the hope that everything would go the way she wanted. Because at that moment Blue was scared stiff.

"Tonight is going to go down in history," Sam announced. "In more ways than one."

Dylan looked up from the bag of ice he was trying to shove into the Bardins' freezer. "Yeah, man. It'll be fun."

"Wow!" Sam said flatly. "Your enthusiasm is overwhelming. I better call the six o'clock news and get a crew over here right away to document your zeal."

"Are you okay, Sam?" Dylan asked.

Sam did a sort of combination frown-snarl. "Why do you ask?"

Dylan shrugged. "You seem a little, uh,

manic or something." Sam had been bouncing from one end of the houseboat to the other for the past couple of hours, talking rapid-fire about the huge bash he was going to have tonight. The guy wasn't out for a fun time—he was on a mission.

Sam ducked past Dylan and pulled a Coke from the fridge. "Manic? Who's manic? I'm simply taking advantage of the fact that both of my parents are away. Is that a crime?"

"No . . . of course not." Dylan gave himself a small (grudging) pat on the back for having encouraged Natalie to stay with Sam. Despite Tanya's words of wisdom on the subject, it was clear to Dylan that Sam needed all the help he could get right now. The guy was on the edge of losing it.

"Good." Sam gulped down approximately half the can of Coke, then burped as if he were participating in a summer camp belching contest. "Now—let's hear some enthusiasm."

Dylan managed to squeeze the ice into the freezer and slammed the door shut. "Dude, I'm totally psyched."

"You should be." Sam set down his can of soda on the tiny kitchen counter and dragged the kitchen table into one corner of the room— he had spent half the morning moving furniture in order to make more room for his potential guests to mingle. "I'm taking measures to ensure that tonight is especially significant in your pathetic life."

"How's that?" Dylan glanced around the kitchen, searching for some task to complete.

He had been happy to help out Sam with party preparations, but being one-on-one with his best friend after everything that had gone down behind the scenes with Natalie was getting harder by the second.

Sam pulled several stacks of plastic cups out of a brown paper grocery bag and tossed them to Dylan. "There are going to be dozens of beautiful girls here tonight—right or wrong?"

"Right," Dylan said. Sam had never had a problem surrounding himself with beautiful women. Until he had decided Natalie was the girl of his dreams, the guy had dated a different girl every week.

Sam grabbed two kitchen chairs and shoved them up against the wall. "One of the babes here tonight is going to have *your* name written on her forehead."

"I hope that's a metaphor . . . or a figure of speech . . . or whatever." When Sam was in one of his out-there moods, anything was possible.

Dylan hadn't seen his best friend so wired since last summer when he discovered that some cable station was threatening to pull *Lost in Space* from its Sunday night lineup.

Or during the winter when Mr. Chaminski had declared that no student was allowed to wear a baseball cap to school or to any school-related event. Forget that Sam didn't watch *Lost in Space* or wear baseball caps—sometimes the energy that brewed beneath his surface needed a target. Apparently he was now focusing all his pent-up anxiety in the direction of tonight's festivities.

Sam plopped onto one of the chairs. "I'm serious, man." He lifted up the bottom of his black T-shirt and wiped a layer of sweat from his forehead.

"What do you mean—serious about what?" Dylan leaned against the refrigerator and crossed his arms in front of his chest in his best male-bonding stance.

"Natalie and I talked about it." As soon as he heard the word *Natalie* Dylan detected a slight ringing in his ears. "We're going to help you find a girl tonight. Someone who can help you brew the old espresso after hours—if you know what I mean."

Small black dots floated in front of Dylan's eyes, and he suddenly felt the need to sit down. No, make that lie down. Natalie wanted to set him up . . . with a girl? What did it mean? The idea of being with anyone but Natalie was too awful to think about. But he had to say something. *Respond*, Dylan ordered himself. *You have to open your mouth and speak.*

"Uh, thanks but no thanks, man. I'm not in the market." There. That had sounded more or less masculine and noncommittal.

"Come on, O'Connor, I'm not buying it."

"I'm *serious*," Dylan insisted. "I don't want to meet anyone."

Sam narrowed his eyes. "Wait a second . . . something is going on here."

"What do you mean?" Dylan's voice was little more than a squeak. Sam was onto him. He knew that Dylan was secretly in love with Natalie, and he planned to beat the blank-blank-blank out of him.

Somewhere in the distance the phone rang. Sam didn't even seem to notice. So much for being saved by the bell.

"You're already interested in someone," Sam said. "Someone specific." He laughed. "I can't believe I didn't think of that before now."

"No, I'm not," Dylan insisted. Wait a second. Maybe this was the wrong tactic. If he went along with Sam's theory, it was entirely possible that his friend would leave him alone and let him pursue this fictional girl in whatever way Dylan saw fit. If not, Sam might spend the entire night attempting to introduce Dylan to every cheerleader in the greater Bay Area.

"You're not?" Sam wiggled his eyebrows.

Dylan coughed. "Or maybe I am—hey, it's none of your business."

Eddie appeared at the doorway of the small kitchen. "Sam, that was Dad on the phone."

Sam clenched his fists. "What did he want?"

Eddie glanced from Sam to Dylan to Sam. "Um, he just wanted to see how everything was going with Mom." He shifted from one foot to the other. "And when I told him we were having a party tonight, he said no way."

Sam raised his eyebrows. "Excuse me?" There was a dark edge to his voice.

"Uh, Dad said we weren't allowed to have a party without at least one of them here. He wanted to talk to you himself, but some guy behind him in line for the pay phone was yelling so loud that Dad finally hung up."

Dylan watched as Sam's fist slammed onto the kitchen table. The bang reverberated throughout the kitchen. Here it was—the nervous energy that had been bubbling within his friend for days. "That jerk!" he screamed. "Who does he think he is?" Sam punched the table again. "The reason there's no parent here is because both Mom and Dad have totally checked out on us." He paused and caught his breath. "From now on, what *I* say goes!"

Dylan looked into his friend's eyes. Sam was on some kind of collision course that spelled big trouble. Dylan needed to forget about Natalie and direct all his attention to keeping Sam from going over the edge. If anything happened tonight to upset Sam's delicate balance, there was no doubt that something bad would occur. Something very, very bad.

## Blue Waxes Nonpoetic About Role Models

Hey, all. I read Tanya's piece about the <u>death</u> <u>of</u> <u>Princess Diana</u>, which I gave a hearty thumbs-up. The ever articulate Ms. Childes got me thinking about the subject of role models in general. The state of American heroes is in pretty sad shape, and I think it's something we all need to think about.

A long time ago, like, in the 1950s, little boys and girls were often asked what they wanted to be when they grew up. Back in those days kids said they wanted to grow up to be the president of the United States or a policewoman or a fireman. Back then kids dreamed of being astronauts and scientists and, yeah, the occasional professional baseball player.

Now, in the 1990s, kids are asked the same question. But no one wants to be a politician anymore. No one cares about NASA or curing cancer. Oh, no. Now all the kids want to be actors or rock stars. Except for the brainy types, of course. The miniature geniuses want to be music producers or TV producers. Everyone else seems interested only in the <u>NBA</u> or the <u>NFL.</u>

Hello, people. The entertainment industry does not comprise all of the United States of America. Let's get real. Let's get deep. Let's turn our backs on Hollywood and start caring about stuff that really matters. Instead of looking to Michael Jordan (not that he isn't a cool guy) and Mariah Carey for our role models, let's turn to good ol' hardworking Mom and Dad. Let's look to our fourth-grade teachers.

If anyone else gives a damn about the state of the world beyond rap music and bad sitcoms, shoot me an <u>e-mail.</u> I'd love to hear from you!

Saturday afternoon Jason studied the dimly lit interior of Celia's garage slash rec room slash den of sin. She had added to the eclectic selection of posters that lined the thin walls. Jason took special note of a life-size poster of Richard Nixon to which Celia had added a mustache and horns. He also noticed that the enormous orange shag carpet that covered much of the cement floor was badly in need of a vacuum job. There were enough crushed Fritos in the rug to bake a macaroni casserole crust.

"I'm thinking of painting a mural in here," Celia said, rising from the shabby couch on which they were lounging. She walked to the far wall of the garage and unceremoniously tore down several Judas Priest posters. "I'm going to paint the Garden of Eden, but Adam and Eve are both going to have mohawks and belly button rings."

"Wow . . . that'll be . . . something." When he had first met Celia, Jason had convinced himself that he found her off-kilter take on the world somewhat alluring. Now she just seemed silly.

# TEN

Celia flipped her hair over one shoulder and did a sort of cat walk back to the sofa. For the millionth time Jason tried to stop himself from comparing his so-called girlfriend to Blue. And for the millionth time it was useless—

*Jason's Mental Checklist*

| Positive | Negative |
|---|---|
| -Celia has beautiful hair. | -Celia's bones are scary-sharp. |
| -Blue has really beautiful hair. | |
| -Blue has a great sense of humor. | -Celia laughs at the oddest times. |
| -Blue understands me—the whole me. | -Celia lives in her own demented world. |
| -Celia wants to be my girlfriend. | -Blue doesn't want to be my girlfriend. |

Why was he even bothering to go over this stuff in his head? Jason knew what he had to do—he had known since the moment he walked out of Dr. Grady's office, filled with newfound resolve.

He turned to Celia, who had picked up a mini–Etch-A-Sketch and now seemed intent on creating an intricate design. "We need to, uh, talk," Jason stuttered.

He wasn't accustomed to saying anything of meaning unless it was compelled by an outside force. Initiating conversation was even more awkward than he had imagined.

Celia slid closer to him on the couch. "Do you *really* want to talk?" she asked, tossing the Etch-A-Sketch to the floor. "Or would you rather do something else?" Her hand was on his bare knee, and the touch of her long nails on his skin sent shivers up his leg.

"Um, we need to talk. For real." Jason cleared his throat. He had seen plenty of breakup scenes in movies, but he had never imagined that he would be the dumper rather than the dumpee.

She leaned forward and kissed him gently on the neck. Then on his cheek just below his earlobe. "Okay, talk." Celia's lips moved to the other side of his face.

Jason bit his lip. It would be so easy to wrap his arms around Celia's waist and pull her close. He had grown accustomed to making out with a beautiful girl on almost a daily basis. Did he really want to give this up?

*With this beautiful girl, yes.*

Jason wrapped his fingers around Celia's wrists and gently moved her hands to a more neutral location. "There's no easy way to do this . . . ," he began. "So I'll just say it."

Every muscle in Celia's body seemed to tense. "Say what?" she asked suspiciously.

A brave man would take the direct approach. But Jason wasn't brave. He was a big, stinking coward. "You know how you move through life thinking that everything is more or less going in the right direction?" he asked. "But then one day you wake up and you realize that you were just taking random steps to fill the emptiness that keeps you awake at night?"

If she was able to understand anything he had just said, Celia was a whole lot brighter than he had given her credit for. "No," she answered. "I have no idea what you're talking about."

So much for the indirect approach. "What I'm trying to say is . . . I mean, what I meant by that was—" Deep breath. *Very* deep breath. "I don'tthinkweshouldseeeachotheranymore." Exhale.

Celia's green eyes were narrowed into dangerous slits. "Excuse me?"

Okay, one more time. Slower. "Celia, you're a great girl . . . but I don't think things are working out between us."

For several moments there was silence. Jason felt the urge to hum a funeral march.

"Is this about Blue?" Celia finally asked, her voice steely.

"Um . . ." Oh, man, he was sure Celia was posing some kind of trick question, but Jason had less than no idea how to respond.

Celia laced her fingers together and cracked each of her knuckles one by one. "You don't have to answer, Jason." Her voice trembled. "You're in love with Blue, aren't you?"

He wanted to issue a denial, but what was the use? Celia would find out the truth eventually. Everyone would. "Yes," he said quietly. "I'm sorry."

Celia nodded. "You never really gave me a chance. . . . You know that, don't you?"

"I know." Dating Celia had been a desperate attempt to force his growing feelings for Blue beneath the surface. But Jason and Celia's relationship (what little there was of it) had been doomed before they ever laid eyes on each other.

Celia sighed deeply. She looked softer now . . . and younger. Jason felt a pang of profound regret. He had never wanted to hurt anyone—especially Celia, who had been the first girl to make him feel like he was actually worthy of achieving boyfriend status.

"Do you mind leaving now?" she asked. "I want to be alone."

Jason reached out to give her a kiss on the cheek, then stopped. What was the point? He stood up. "Thanks, Celia . . . for everything."

She didn't respond. What could he expect her to say, anyway? He slipped out the small door at the side of the garage and stepped into the bright afternoon sunlight. He was free now. Free to embark on the most terrifying adventure of his life thus far.

Before this day was over, Jason was going to tell Blue O'Connor the truth. He was going to declare his love.

San Francisco Memorial Hospital seemed significantly less ominous this afternoon. Now that his mother was safely tucked away in rehab, Sam didn't feel the burning fear of death as he strode through the enormous automatic doors of the emergency room. Nonetheless, he hoped that after he dealt with his mom's insurance papers, he would never have to come inside this place again.

Sam walked to the admittance desk, where just a few nights ago he had been so terrorized by Nurse Jane Stanton. Thank goodness someone else was sitting behind the huge round desk this afternoon.

"May I help you?" The woman's voice was pleasant and friendly, but Sam could see the same weariness in her eyes that he had seen in Ms. Stanton's.

"I'm here about Margaret Bardin. The hospital said I had to fill out some forms or something." *Cups. Check. Anything in the houseboat remotely valuable hidden away. Check. Potato chips and pretzels. Check. Stereo speakers on deck. Check.* Sam's mind was far from insurance forms and hospitals—which was exactly where he wanted it to be.

The nurse typed something into her computer. A moment later she handed Sam a clipboard—attached to which was a sheaf of papers an inch thick. "Fill those out and return them to me."

Sam groaned. "You're joking, right?" He would be here until tomorrow morning if he went through each one of these.

The nurse shook her head. "'Fraid not, hon. That's procedure."

Another groan. Man, a child doing the parent stuff wasn't just traumatic—it was also incredibly tedious. "Do you at least have a pen I could borrow?" he asked.

She shook her head again, holding up the ballpoint pen in her hand. "Sorry, I had to steal this one from one of the nurses."

Sam turned away from the desk and headed for the waiting room. He'd have to bum a pen there. So far this little excursion to the hospital wasn't exactly getting him in a party mood.

"Hi, Sam."

Sam glanced to his left. And found a very attractive girl standing in front of him. Unfortunately he had absolutely no idea what her name was. "Uh, hi . . ."

She grinned. "I'm Hallie. We met the other night over bad coffee and stale doughnuts."

"Hallie Barnett!" Now that she had put herself into context, Sam totally remembered her.

He also remembered that Hallie had looked significantly different the other night. Instead of braids her hair was brushed long and loose and shiny. Behind her small, wire-rimmed glasses Sam saw that Hallie's eyes were deep ocean blue. Tonight Hallie was wearing a short dress that showed off her slim legs. The girl he had met in the lounge had been cute, but *this* girl was a knockout, plain and simple.

"Don't tell me your mom is back again," Hallie said. Her eyes radiated the warmth and understanding of a person who knew what it felt like to have one's world blown to small, sharp bits.

Sam shook his head. "She's in rehab." He was surprised how easy it was to share that particular piece of information with Hallie. Until now he had planned to tell everyone but the gang at the café that his mom was on an extended vacation in Arizona or the Bahamas. "How's your dad doing?"

The light in Hallie's eyes dimmed. "His diabetes has gotten so bad that the doctors say he has to have dialysis once a week." She pointed toward the ceiling. "He's upstairs having it done right now. I thought I might as well come down here and say hi to the nurses. They know me by now."

Sam grimaced. He didn't know much about dialysis—but he knew that it was a painful and nasty process that involved having tubes stuck in one's arm for an extended period of time. He could only imagine what it was like for Hallie to watch her dad go through something like that.

"I'm sorry, Hallie." This girl was little more than a stranger, but Sam felt an overwhelming urge to wrap his arms around her.

She shrugged. "Hey, at least he's alive, right?"

"Right." *But for how long?* Sam asked silently.

She held out a black Bic pen. "I heard you say you're short one of these bad boys."

He took the Bic. "Thanks." Man, this girl was amazing. She was in the middle of a major life crisis, and she still had the presence of mind to worry about the fact that Sam was pen challenged.

"You can keep it," Hallie offered. "By the time you're done filling out all of those forms, there probably won't be much ink left, anyway."

"Thanks again. I owe you one." Sam knew the conversation had reached its natural conclusion, but still he wanted to keep talking to Hallie.

"Well, I guess I better go check on my dad," Hallie said. "We've got another exciting evening of *America's Most Wanted* and *Unsolved Mysteries* ahead of us."

That sounded deadly dull. Sam had a better idea. "Don't spend the whole night baby-sitting your father," he said firmly. "I'm having a party at my houseboat . . . no sick or dysfunctional parents allowed."

"I don't know. . . ." Hallie's voice trailed off.

"Please," Sam said. "I'd love to have a fellow hospital groupie there to keep me company while I listen to some jerk complain about how hard his life is now that his parents won't agree to pay for a vacation in Hawaii."

Hallie laughed. "When you put it like that, how can I refuse?"

"You can't." As Sam studied Hallie's kind face he had another great idea.

Hallie was the perfect girl for Dylan. She was beautiful, sweet, responsible, and something else that he couldn't quite name yet. Something special.

"You're going to have an awesome time tonight," Sam promised.

Hallie laughed again. "You're a nice guy, Sam Bardin."

Suddenly Sam felt ready to tackle the universe—and the stack of papers on his clipboard. Now all he had to do was get out of this horrible hospital as quickly as possible so that he could go home and call Natalie. If anyone knew how to go about making a love match, it would be his girlfriend. He couldn't wait to tell her that he'd found the perfect girl for Dylan.

"Do you want to wear my pink silk shirt?" Mia's voice sounded curiously sincere.

Natalie spun around. She had been staring at herself in her full-length mirror for the last fifteen minutes. She had selected a pair of tight black pants (thong definitely mandatory) and high platform heels to wear to

Sam's party. But her top half was still bare except for the new flesh-toned Wonderbra she had bought during her lunch break.

"Mia!" Natalie instinctively reached for a T-shirt. She had no desire for any sort of sisterly comparison of her and Mia's respective bra sizes to go on while she was sans shirt. "Have you ever heard of knocking?"

Mia held out a sixteen-ounce bottle of diet Coke. "Hey, I come in peace, complete with a carbonated olive branch."

Natalie pulled on one of the many white Hanes T-shirts she had permanently borrowed from her dad's top dresser drawer. "Oh . . . well, thanks."

Mia crossed the pale pink wall-to-wall carpet that covered Natalie's bedroom floor and sank delicately into the chaise longue that Mr. van Lenton had given Natalie for her sixteenth birthday. "You really can borrow my pink shirt—it would look great with your dark hair."

"Um . . . maybe. I'll think about it." Natalie sat down on her bed, seized with an acute sense of discomfort.

Ever since Natalie had discovered that her mother was alive, she and Mia had been walking on eggshells around each other. At first Natalie had been furious with Mia for not revealing immediately the fact that she had discovered months earlier that Delia was alive. And then the sisters had reached a tentative truce. It was hard to stay angry with the only person in the world who was in the same exact boat as you.

"Have you heard from Delia?" Mia asked.

"An e-mail," Natalie responded. She picked up the nail file she had been using earlier and went to work on the pinkie nail she had bitten off during this afternoon's *Ricki Lake* show about cheating girlfriends. "And I, uh, wrote her a letter."

Mia nodded. "Same here."

For once they had something in common. Natalie wasn't sure what to do with that bit of information. "Do you think she loves us?" Natalie asked. She couldn't help herself. It was a question that had been rolling over and over in her head since she and Dylan had returned from Portland.

Mia didn't say anything right away. She picked up Natalie's hairbrush and ran it through her long auburn hair, making the already shiny mane gleam as if her tresses had just been waxed and buffed. "I think she does love us," Mia said finally. "But in her own way."

Natalie sighed. "Love doesn't make a lot of sense, does it?" Her thoughts had drifted past Delia now. Lately it seemed that every conversation she started ended with the same question. Sam or Dylan? Dylan or Sam?

"You're not talking about Mom anymore, are you?" Mia asked. Apparently she hadn't been admitted to Stanford University based on her superior good looks alone.

Natalie shrugged. "None of your business."

Mia tossed the brush onto Natalie's bed. "Jeez, Nat. The amount of hostility you have toward me is awe inspiring. Here I am, trying to fulfill my role as concerned big sister, and all you can say is 'none of your business.'"

Natalie glanced at her sister. Mia looked genuinely concerned—even her toothpaste ad smile had disappeared. "I'm sorry, Mia . . . but it's hard for me to look at you like some guardian angel big sis who's always handing out words of wisdom to her one and only sibling."

"I'm not your enemy, Nat." Mia stared out the window for a moment. "Listen, you were there for me when I was in the hospital—when I had anorexia."

Natalie flinched. She hated talking about that time in her sister's life. It was *so* uncomfortable. "That's different. . . ."

"I want to be here for you, Natalie. Tell me what's on your mind." Mia's voice was so serious that Natalie could *almost* forget the fact that her sister floated through life (anorexia aside) in a haze of self-confidence and self-love.

Natalie took a deep breath. She had to talk to *someone*. Tanya was the usual victim—but she was so caught up in her own minidrama that she didn't have much leftover brainpower to deal with anyone else's traumas. "I'm going out with

Sam," Natalie said quietly. "But I'm in love with someone else."

"Dylan." It wasn't a question—it was a statement.

"Yeah . . . Dylan." Natalie couldn't believe that she was revealing her innermost secrets to her sister, but here it was. She was doing just that.

"Can I offer a piece of advice without having my head bitten off?" Mia asked.

Natalie had to smile. Despite her basic contempt for Mia, she had to admit that her older sister knew her better than most other people on the planet. "You can try."

"Follow your heart," Mia said. "If you and Dylan love each other, then there's no way you're going to stay away from each other forever." She stood up. "The longer you keep up this charade with Sam, the more he's going to hurt when he finds out the truth."

"I don't know. . . ." Mia was making a certain amount of sense—objectively. But there was a big part of Natalie who tended to want to do the opposite of whatever her sister thought was the proper course of action.

Mia walked across the bedroom and stopped at the door. "Trust me, Nat. You're not helping Sam by pretending to be in love with him." She reached out and patted Natalie on the shoulder. "Now—I'm going to go get that pink shirt. It'll be perfect."

Natalie watched Mia disappear down the hall.

She wasn't used to having heart-to-heart rap sessions with her sister. But even in her most defiant little sister mode, she had to admit that Mia was making at least a tiny bit of sense.

Natalie pictured herself walking into Sam's party in the awesome pink shirt. Maybe there was hope for some actual sisterhood after all. Maybe. . . .

## Chef Natalie's Advice on the Following Subject:
## How to Bake a Successful Birthday Cake—
## No Matter What Your Cooking Handicap

Let's be honest, people. A lot of you haven't spent much time in the kitchen. When you're hungry, you pop a Lean Cuisine into the microwave, pour a bowl of cereal, or smother a bagel in cream cheese. But there do exist those special occasions when we want to show a friend that yes, they're worth the effort of donning that apron and delving into the world of pots and pans.

I'll cut to the chase. I'm talking birthday cakes here. Don't believe those heartless souls who out of sheer laziness insist that the store-bought cake is just as good as something created by *your* loving hands. I'm not suggesting that Joe Blow needs a double German chocolate cake. But a little effort goes a long way in this department.

So here's what I suggest: Stay focused. Your goal is to bake a cake, add some frosting, and get your friends to sing a rousing rendition of the happy birthday song. Don't kid yourself into thinking that you're going to bake some amazing cake from a recipe in your mom's (or dad's) favorite cookbook. Instead take the road more traveled. *Buy a mix!*

That's right, folks. Go to your local Safeway and purchase a nice box of Duncan Hines or Betty Crocker. Don't go for the double chocolate or the angel food. Stick with vanilla—trust me, it's always a crowd pleaser. And then all you have to do is read the back of the box and add a couple of eggs, water, and whatever else the so-called recipe calls for.

Now, if you want to ensure that your birthday guests ooh and aah over your creation, take this tip to heart: *Add an extra stick of butter!*

Bake and enjoy. And don't forget to spread frosting on the cake and write "Happy birthday _____ (fill in name here)" in icing.

"Where do you go to school?" Dylan shouted over the Nine Inch Nails album that was blasting from the stereo in the Bardins' small living room.

Hallie Barnett leaned closer and pointed to her ear. "What?" she shouted.

"Where do you go to *school?*" Dylan screamed. This was ridiculous. There was less than no possibility for normal conversation with the decibel level of the music in the houseboat.

"Sunset Hill!" Hallie shouted back.

Interesting. Sunset Hill was an all-girls private school downtown. Dylan hadn't put Hallie in the rich girl category. "Do you like it?" he shouted.

"No!" Hallie screamed. "The girls are all—" Suddenly the music stopped. "—snobs," she yelled.

Dylan laughed. Man, it was nice to be able to hear his own thoughts for a moment. "I guess you feel pretty strongly about that."

Hallie had turned a very becoming light pink color. "Sorry . . . I wasn't prepared for the silence."

"I know the feeling." Pause. And yet another pause. Clearly he had to say something that resembled polite party talk. But beyond the basic how-old-are-you and where-do-you-go-to-school questions, his mind was blank.

Five minutes ago Sam had planted Dylan in front of Hallie and told him to "go for it." Now Dylan was expected to entertain a total stranger who didn't know one other person at the party. If only Sam weren't on this random kick to get Dylan a girlfriend. There was nothing worse than having the boyfriend of the girl one loved trying to set you up on a date.

"Um . . . where do you live?" Dylan finally asked Hallie. Duh.

Hallie grinned. "You know, Dylan, you don't have to stand here and talk to me for the rest of the night just because Sam told you to."

"Oh, no . . . I mean, uh . . . I don't know what you're talking about." Well, she was certainly direct. And she was pretty. But Hallie wasn't Natalie, and that made her ultimately unqualified to fill the role of Dylan's girlfriend.

Hallie shifted from one foot to the other, looking slightly nervous. "Can we cut the bull for a second?"

"Uh, sure." She was really, *really* direct.

"Who is that girl?" Hallie pointed across the room at a beautiful dark-haired girl who was laughing.

It took almost three seconds for Dylan to

register the fact that the girl was Natalie. She was wearing a pair of very tight black pants and a pale pink silk shirt that made her skin look as if it were lit from within. She was breathtaking. "Um . . . that's Natalie van Lenton."

"Who is she?" Hallie asked.

Wow, what a question. *She's the girl of my dreams. She's the most wonderful, sensitive person on the planet. She's . . . Natalie.* "She's, uh, Sam's girlfriend."

"Oh." Hallie's face fell. "I guess that's why I've seen him staring at her for the past hour."

"Yeah . . . I guess so." Poor, innocent Hallie had no idea that she had just driven a knife straight through Dylan's heart. He accepted the fact that Sam and Natalie were a couple—he was even struggling valiantly to *embrace* the notion. But he didn't want to hear about the relationship more than was absolutely necessary. . . . It was just too hard.

"I should have known Sam had a girlfriend—he's too great a guy to be available." Hallie was still staring at Natalie with a wistful expression on her face.

Slowly—or not so slowly—Dylan was starting to get the picture. Hallie had a crush on Sam. "Yeah, well . . . you never know what might happen. They could break up." Okay, so that was wishful thinking. But hey, it *was* possible that Sam and Natalie could break up—eventually.

Hallie turned her attention back to Dylan.

"Thanks for acting as my party guide tonight, but if you don't mind, I think I'm going to take off."

Dylan recognized the tone in her voice—pure heartbreak. "Okay, sure."

He watched as Hallie negotiated her way through the crowded living room. He wished someone could tell him exactly why it was that nothing in life ever went according to plan. In an ideal world there would be two guys and two girls, and each of the guys would be in love with one of the girls and vice versa. There would be no complications. Instead everyone always seemed to be in love with the same person, or the wrong person, or no one at all.

Dylan sighed. Hallie deserved to be happy. He deserved to be happy. Sam and Natalie deserved to be happy. But as of this moment only one of them—Sam—was actually happy. And his happiness was totally distorted by the fact that his father was in jail and his mother was in rehab. There was no logic to it . . . no logic at all.

"Hey, gorgeous, you know you'd look even prettier if you were smiling." A short guy wearing a Surf Naked T-shirt leered at Tanya.

"Oh, yeah, well, why should I be smiling?" she asked. Why did God create guys like this? As far as Tanya could tell, obnoxious males occupied no meaningful place on the food chain.

He grinned—at which point Tanya noted that a small piece of a tortilla chip was caught between the guy's front teeth. "Because of me." He laughed. "Because now that I found you, I'm gonna spend the rest of the night with you. Now doesn't that make you feel like grinning?"

"The only thing that makes me feel like doing is finding a big old machete, chopping off your ugly mug, and sticking your severed head on a hot poker." She batted her eyelashes. "Anything else you'd like to chat about?"

"Uh, maybe later." Surf Naked guy melted into the Bardins' crowded kitchen.

"Happy hunting," Tanya called after him.

She pressed up against the wall of the narrow hallway that connected the kitchen to the stairs that led to the houseboat's upper deck. Tanya wasn't sure she had ever seen so many teenagers packed into one dwelling before.

"Great party, huh?" Love Rheingold (the daughter of ex-hippie parents and a fellow Alta Vista soon-to-be senior) yelled into Tanya's ear.

"Sure. Great." Tanya nodded and made all the right kind of smiles.

Much to Tanya's relief, Love moved past her and toward the stairs. Tanya had to admit that by almost anyone's standard, this party was a huge success. People were dancing, shouting, making out on various sofas, and generally causing mayhem.

But Tanya was wallowing in her own personal hell. Life without Major was truly miserable.

"Where's Major? Did you two break up or what?" As if on cue, Vanessa Elison had appeared at Tanya's side. The girl was truly a menace to society. She had an uncanny ability to say exactly the wrong thing at exactly the wrong time.

"I don't know—or care—where Major Johnson is tonight," Tanya informed Vanessa. "And FYI, we were never *going out* in the first place." *Sure, I was—am—madly in love with the guy, but we were never actually an official couple. Thanks to him.*

Vanessa tipped her glass of punch to her mouth. "Too bad, Tanya. He was bee-u-tiful."

*Don't remind me.* "If you like him so much, give him a call." Tanya scanned the crowded hallway for a familiar face. Unfortunately each and every one of her friends seemed to have vanished. She was trapped.

"Maybe I will." Vanessa gave Tanya a little cheerleader kind of wave and squeezed past.

Tanya desperately needed fresh air, but she wasn't about to trail Vanessa up the stairs to the deck. "Maybe I *should* have called Jackson," Tanya muttered. She had thought the fact that she had decided to face this party alone—rather than arm in arm with a gorgeous (if tremendously boring) guy—was a sign of big-time personal progress. Now she decided the fact made her just plain lonely.

*Remember your resolution,* Tanya told herself. *No more men. Period.* She had vowed to herself that she was going to abstain from any romantic dealings with the male half of the species in favor of pursuing one of her many fledgling hobbies.

"Natalie . . . I need Natalie," Tanya said aloud. "Or Blue. Or Dylan, who's probably even more miserable than I am at this particular moment." Great. Now she was talking to herself in a hallway that was literally busting with people.

Aha! Tanya saw that the previously full kitchen had emptied out. She focused on the door of the refrigerator and elbowed her way past a couple who were using the hallway as if it were a roomy backseat in a four-door sedan. PDA really needed to be outlawed. At last Tanya found herself alone in the kitchen. "Freedom!" she declared.

And then Tanya moved her head about thirty degrees to the right. *No. . . .* Her jaw dropped to the floor (at least it would have dropped to the floor if it had been that extraordinarily long). Faith, The Girl, was standing not ten feet away from her.

Tanya blinked. It was late, and she was tired and bumming. She was probably just imagining that she saw Faith—it wasn't possible that the girl was actually here, in Sam's houseboat.

Faith. The name left a foul taste in Tanya's mouth—sort of a bile-vomit combo. This wasn't happening. This could *not* be happening. Only it *was* happening. Tanya would have recognized Major's live-in girlfriend if she were blindfolded and lit on fire. And Faith was holding hands with a very cute Asian guy who definitely was *not* Major Johnson.

Tanya closed the distance between them. "What are you doing here?" she yelled at her.

"I—we saw the flyer for the party at @café," Faith stammered.

"Jeez, girl, you have some nerve." Tanya's entire being was subsumed by deep, abiding rage.

Faith looked utterly shocked. "Um . . . I don't—"

"Shut up!" Tanya barked. "I can't believe you had the audacity to show up here, period. But to bring another *guy*. That's simply . . . inexcusable."

"What?" Faith looked like a rat cornered by a gigantic alley cat.

And then it registered. Faith didn't know who Tanya was. She had absolutely no idea that the girl standing in front of her was the same girl from whom she had stolen Major.

"I happen to be a close, personal friend of Major Johnson's," Tanya spat out. "And I cannot *believe* that you're cheating on him with lover boy here. You're the worst kind of scum there is."

"I'm Faith Lariviere." Faith gave Tanya a

penetrating look. "But I didn't steal *anyone* from *anyone*."

Lariviere? What kind of stupid last name was that? *Exotic. Beautiful. Sexy.* "Don't even try it, *Faith*. I have you totally figured out."

"Let me guess," Faith said. She was smiling now, which made Tanya ten times more furious. "You're Tanya Childes."

"Damn right I am." Tanya looked over Faith's shoulder, still half expecting to see Major's beautiful, smug face behind her. But no one was there. At least no one who even somewhat resembled the lying, thoughtless jerk who had made Tanya's life barely worth living.

"He's not here," Faith said. "I'm alone. Well, I'm not *alone*, but I mean, I'm not here with Major. He doesn't even know there's a party here tonight."

"Why are you here?" Tanya asked. "And why are you cheating on Major?" She paused. "That is just *so* low."

"I *was* here simply to have a good time," Faith answered. "But judging from your reaction to me, I think it's lucky we ran into each other."

This girl got better and better. Or worse and worse, depending on how one looked at it. "Is there a point to this discussion?" Tanya asked. "Or are you in my face solely to lord over me the fact that I failed where you succeeded?"

Tanya had never before felt such hatred toward another human being. If only there was something wrong with the girl, Tanya might not have felt such an acute need to crush Faith's diet Coke can against her perfect forehead. Jeans weren't supposed to look that good on a girl under five-eight. And what was up with her tank top? The thing looked as if it had been sewed onto Faith's body in the dressing room of Urban Outfitters.

"Can you drop the attitude for just a sec?" Faith asked.

For once in her life Tanya was speechless. She had no idea how to respond to Faith's question. As for dropping her attitude—there was zero chance. "I'm sure you're aware of the First Amendment," Tanya said. "Say whatever you want."

"Now that we're, uh, chatting, I want to talk to you about Major," Faith said in a relatively pleasant tone. "What you *think* is going on with him and me isn't actually going on."

"Whatever." This girl was a serious sicko. Did she get her kicks from going around tormenting the girls who she crushed in her path?

"I'm serious, Tanya."

She did look a bit subdued. Tanya had been ready to bolt from the kitchen, but now she leaned against the counter and tried to look casual. "Like I said, say whatever it is you want to say."

"Major and I are just friends," Faith said quickly. "Yes, I've been staying at his apartment—but not for the reason you think."

"I see." Tanya's heart beat slightly faster in her chest. Was it possible that—? No, not possible. *Don't even go there, girl,* Tanya cautioned herself.

"Major's mom is my godmother," Faith continued. "My mom and his mom went to the University of Indiana together—"

"Your family history is fascinating," Tanya interrupted. "But I have a lot of people I need to talk to. . . ."

"Listen," Faith urged. "Just listen to what I have to say." When Tanya didn't say anything, Faith seemed to rev up for a prolonged discussion about her various Johnson family dealings. "See, I go to UC Berkeley on scholarship. And I work part-time to pay for my housing and stuff." She paused. "Anyway, the apartment above mine had a leak a couple of weeks ago and flooded my place. I lost everything I own."

"Harsh." Despite herself Tanya experienced a flash of sympathy. Faith was a low-down, man-stealing chick, but no one deserved to have their apartment trashed.

"Major offered to let me stay at his place until I could save up some money," Faith continued. "I sleep on the couch."

"Oh." Tanya wasn't sure what to do with this new information. "Why didn't Major just tell me that when I saw him? What's the big secret?"

Faith rolled her eyes. "There's *no* secret— that's what I'm trying to tell you." She stood on her tiptoes and kissed the guy Tanya had labeled in her mind as The Other Man. "This is my boyfriend—of several months—Marcus."

"Oh." Tanya felt like a fool. Faith was obviously a basically nice person who had become the unwitting target of Tanya's misplaced venom. But Faith's revelation didn't change the fundamental misery of Tanya's life. Major hadn't cared enough about Tanya to track her down and tell her the truth. He had let her walk out the door—no questions asked.

"Listen . . . thanks for telling me about all this," Tanya said. "But it's clear that Major doesn't want a relationship with me." She paused to swallow the giant lump that had formed in her throat.

Faith took a step closer to Tanya and rested her hand on Tanya's shoulder. "Major is in love with you, Tanya. I know he is."

"Don't make me laugh." *Ha, ha, ha.* "He's told me a hundred times that he has no intention of making any kind of commitment to me—that's true regardless of whether or not you two are a couple."

"I know what he *said*," Faith declared. "He told me the whole story after you stormed out of the apartment the other day. The poor guy was so torn up that he blabbed every gory detail."

"He did?" Major wasn't the "sharing" type. This new side of his personality was interesting—at the very least.

Faith nodded. "The guy is stubborn, he's

annoying, and he's confused. He also happens to be in love with you—whether or not he's willing to admit it to himself."

"I . . . I, uh, don't know what to say." Tanya's head was spinning. She felt like bowing down and kissing Faith's feet.

"Talk to Major," Faith urged. "Don't let him drive you away—stick in there." She nudged Marcus in the side. "Let's go, babe."

They disappeared down the hall, and Tanya sank into one of the kitchen chairs. She had never been a person who backed away from challenges—and now wasn't the time to start running scared. As soon as she recovered from the initial shock of Faith's words, Tanya would blow off the party and search out Major. It was time they had a talk—because if Major really did love Tanya . . . then both of their worlds were about to be turned upside down.

BACK      FORWARD      HOME      STOP

LINK:

## Jason Discusses Fall Fashions
## (Just Kidding)
## Really, Jason Talks About Taoism

Okay, I'm no religion expert. To be totally honest, I haven't even been to church since I was confirmed (whatever that means) at the age of thirteen. And I have a healthy skepticism toward anything that falls under the category of "institutional." But there's a lot to be said for what each and every religion/philosophy has to say.

I've always shunned Buddhism—mostly because Richard Gere is the American poster boy for a much respected Asian tradition. But I digress. Let's move past Richard Gere and talk about Taoism.

Here's the deal: This really wise guy named Lao-tze wrote an amazing book called the Tao Te Ching. Lao-tze talked about human potential and how we're all "uncarved blocks."

I'm not going to pretend that I understand Taoism on any profound level, but I think there's a lot to be said for following the Tao, also known as the Way. In other words, go with the flow. But don't go with the flow in any old way that seems convenient. Go with the flow of the universe.

Remove your thoughts from the materialism of the modern world and focus on your inner sense of integrity. Instead of stressing out about whether or not you get into an Ivy League college (not that there's anything wrong with Harvard and Yale), worry about your next-door neighbor, your community, your city.

I'm not making much sense—and I don't even know if I'm accurately portraying the ideas of Lao-tze and Taoism—but I'm trying to send a basic message that I think (in my oh-so-humble opinion) has some merit.

This is it: Be true to yourself—your *real* self. Tap into the uncarved block that lives inside you—even if that means tuning out sneaker commercials and slasher film trailers.

Let's all move on to a higher, wiser plane, where we care more about truth and justice and all that good stuff than we do about the right kind of clothes or the right CDs or the right girl on our arm. Let's care about stuff that *matters.*

Natalie stared into Sam's nearly empty refrigerator. Aha! There was one can of lemon-lime seltzer hidden behind a limp head of iceberg lettuce. Natalie reached for the soda. "Proof of God is all around us," she murmured, anticipating the feel of the cold liquid sliding down her throat.

It was almost midnight, and her voice was shot. She had been yelling at the top of her lungs for the past three hours in order to be heard over the general noise of the party. At most parties Natalie would have retreated to a safe corner of a sofa by this hour and passed the evening chatting with whoever happened by her perch.

But this wasn't most parties— as Sam's girlfriend, Natalie was expected to behave as a de facto hostess. Which basically meant that she had to patrol the houseboat and make sure that nobody was causing major permanent damage.

"Hey, Nat."

"Dylan . . . hi." They had barely spoken to each other since the

**TWELVE**

party kicked off around eight o'clock. She had even managed, sort of, to push Sam's matchmaking plan to the back of her mind. But now that Dylan was here—standing just inches from her—Natalie found herself slightly breathless. She shut the refrigerator door, taking slow, deep breaths.

"You've been quite the police sergeant tonight," he commented. "I admired you from a distance as you threw out those two guys who were using the Bardins' TV set as a punching bag."

Natalie rolled her eyes. "Why didn't you help me? I thought that tall guy was going to rip my arm out of its socket when I tried to drag him away from the girl he was ogling."

Dylan laughed. "I'm sorry, I should have come to your rescue—but I was enjoying watching you too much to intervene."

Natalie's heart beat a little faster. Dylan's voice had deepened as he uttered the word *watching*. All of a sudden she felt like a character in a movie who was engaging in some kind of dangerous flirtation with the man who everybody knew was all wrong for her. Except that Dylan wasn't wrong for her. He was totally, totally right in every way.

*Remember Sam.* How many times had she said those words to herself over the past several days? Dozens. "So, uh, did you have any luck tonight?" Natalie asked.

"Luck? What do you mean?" Dylan leaned against the counter and crossed his arms in front of his chest.

Natalie had seen him wear that same green button-down shirt a hundred times, but she had never noticed before how the color turned his eyes from a deep blue to an aqua green. She had also never noticed the fact that a slight stubble shadowed Dylan's cheeks late at night. Despite herself Natalie longed to feel his rough cheek against her skin. "Uh, you know, luck with all the pretty girls here tonight."

Was she really saying this stuff? *You have no right to be jealous. No right at all.*

"I'm not looking for luck," Dylan said quietly. He stared into her eyes. "I'm looking for a miracle."

Something inside her melted. *Keep your distance. Stay focused.* "Well, it seemed to me like you were having a pretty good time talking to Sam's friend Hallie."

She shouldn't have said that. Natalie *knew* she shouldn't have said that. But some outside force had taken over her being and forced her to spew out that nasty, petty comment. Jeez, she was only human.

Dylan shrugged. Had shoulders in the act of shrugging ever been so sexy? Natalie seriously doubted it. "She talked. I talked. It was nothing."

There was something in his voice. . . . He was holding back. Natalie was sure of it. "Okay, out with it."

He raised his eyebrows. "Out with what?"

This interaction had the distinct ring of game playing. Natalie rolled the dice. "You liked her, didn't you? I could tell." She held her breath. *Please say no. Please say you thought she was the most revolting creature you ever laid eyes on.*

"Hallie is a very attractive girl—there's no denying that."

"Nope. No denying that." Natalie felt like barfing.

"We had an interesting conversation," Dylan continued. His gaze hadn't wavered—he was still staring into Natalie's eyes as if he were checking out a new zit in a mirror. Okay, that was a bad comparison, but the point was that he was looking at her *intensely.*

"Tell me about it." If he had asked her out, Natalie was going to lie down and die. She couldn't take it. She simply couldn't accept the thought of Dylan with another girl. Not now . . . not after she had loved him secretly for so, so long.

Dylan laughed. "The interesting part had nothing to do with me, Nat."

"Oh . . . really?" *Keep it casual.* She had to pretend like a huge wave of relief hadn't just washed over her. Dylan was entitled to date whoever he wanted—Natalie had no right to intervene in any way, shape, or form.

He nodded. "I got the definite feeling that Hallie has a crush on Sam."

"Oh." Natalie was appalled by the fact that this particular bit of information elicited no feeling within herself aside from sheer gratitude that the crush was on Sam rather than Dylan.

For a few long seconds neither of them said a word. At least neither of them said a word *out loud*. The great Unspoken was flying back and forth between them at a rapid rate of speed.

"I'm, uh, going to dig up some more CDs from Sam's room," Dylan said eventually. "I was on my way when I ran into you."

"I'll help you get 'em." The words were out of her mouth before she even thought them.

"Great!" Dylan responded—equally quickly.

Natalie felt as if she were walking through a dream—a dream where she got away with doing really bad things—as she followed Dylan out of the kitchen. She kept her eyes glued to the spot just between his shoulder blades as they made their way through the crowded hallway that led to Sam's tiny bedroom. Not that there was anything technically wrong with her joining Dylan in a quest for CDs.

When they arrived at the door of the bedroom, Natalie half expected to find some couple lying on top of one of the bunk beds, furiously making out. But the room was empty. Natalie took one tentative step inside the room.

"Maybe we should shut the door," Dylan said. "You know, just to make sure that a bunch of people don't come barging in here with their own ideas about what the musical selection should be."

"Yeah . . . I mean, that's a good idea." Natalie kicked the door shut. In her peripheral vision she was keenly aware of a black plastic CD tower in the corner of the room. She knew that the correct course of action was to walk right over to the tower and begin choosing a new selection of CDs.

But Natalie didn't move. And neither did Dylan. He was giving her this . . . look. The CD tower seemed to vaporize. The bunk beds, the dresser, and the nightstand seemed to fade away. Except for Dylan and Natalie the room was just four walls and a closed door.

"Nat. . . ." His voice was ragged.

"Dylan." She wasn't sure if she had uttered his name aloud or simply said it in her mind.

He took a step. She took a step. Only a foot of navy blue carpet separated their bodies. *Please, let it happen.* A kiss was imminent. She knew that with every fiber of her being. Natalie had never wanted something so much in her whole life.

And then Dylan was standing right in front of her. She tilted her head and found herself staring at the shape of his full, dark red lips. "Dylan . . . ," she whispered. This time she knew she had spoken out loud.

He reached out and placed his hands on her forearms. Slowly, so slowly he moved his hands up the length of her arms. A million shivers shot out from her arms and traveled through each and every inch of her body. Finally Dylan's hands came to rest on her shoulders.

"I love you, Dylan." She had never said that to him before. And she shouldn't be saying it now. But a force had taken control of her.

"I love you, Nat." He pulled her toward him, moving one hand from her shoulder to her cheek.

And then their lips met. Natalie shut her eyes, shut her mind, shut her conscience. Her whole world consisted of Dylan's lips and his hands. She smelled the fresh, clean scent of his soap and felt the taut muscles of his back beneath her hands.

Images of Sam flashed through her mind, then slipped away. Next she saw Hallie's face, laughing and smiling at Dylan. And finally, finally there was nothing but those soft lips and strong hands.

Dylan's lips moved from her lips to her ear. "I can't help myself," he whispered.

"I know," Natalie whispered back. "I know."

She pulled his head back toward her lips, and they kissed again.

*Forgive me,* Natalie pleaded silently to Sam. *This is bigger than both of us.* And it was. Dylan was everything. And Natalie simply didn't have the strength to turn away.

She was a woman in love . . . and nothing was going to keep her away from the object of her desire.

Jason stood at the door of the Bardins' tiny den, guarding his spot with a vigilance and aggression that he hadn't known he was capable of. But he had waited almost two hours for the den to clear out—he wasn't about to let anyone else inside. He needed this room all to himself. The second he caught sight of Blue walking down the hallway, he was going to pull her inside and force her to hear him out.

Hours had passed since Jason had arrived at Sam's party one hundred percent resolved to confess all to Blue. But his immediate plans had been foiled by the unexpected—and unfortunate—presence of Christian Sands. Jason hadn't been prepared for Blue to bring an actual date to the party. He had been even *less* prepared for the sight of Christian and Blue dancing to Sam's *Boogie Nights* sound track. But Jason wasn't going to allow himself to back down just because Christian was around.

And then he saw her. Blue was walking down the narrow hallway, her light brown shoulder-length hair swinging from side to side as she twisted and turned between the many bodies in her path. Jason's mouth went dry, and his heart pounded painfully. This was it.

"Blue!" His voice cracked as he called her name.

She stepped out from behind a guy whose neck was the size of the trunk of an oak tree. "Jason . . . hey."

Instead of the overalls Blue usually wore, she had put on a long, formfitting white sundress, complete with spaghetti straps. And she had chosen white platform heels instead of the black Dr. Marten sandals he saw her in almost every day. She was, in a word, smokin'.

"You got a minute?" He managed to get out the whole sentence without another crack in his voice.

"Sure," Blue answered. She stepped around a couple who were making out next to the door of the den and walked inside.

Jason quickly shut the door behind her. If anyone tried to come inside, he planned to smash their nose into their face. At least that's what he would have planned to do if he knew anything about kicking butt. As it was, he just planned to lean against the door and pray that nobody tried to come in.

"Have a seat." Jason pointed to the sofa.

Blue gave Jason what he interpreted as a strange look and plunked down on the couch. "Good party, huh?"

"Yeah . . . if you like drunk guys threatening to pick you up and toss you into the ocean."

Blue was silent for a moment. "Are you okay?"

He leaned heavily against the door. "Who, me? Fine. Fine." He ignored a soft knocking sound from outside in the hall. "Why do you, uh, ask?" Damn. There was that crack again.

"You look sort of . . . wired." Blue leaned against the back of the sofa and seemed to wait for some kind of coherent response to her observations.

Jason felt wired. More than wired. He felt like he had a million volts of electricity pumping through him. "Too much java, I guess," he answered lamely.

"Okay. . . ." She was looking at him like she thought he should be checked into the nearest loony bin pronto.

"I have something to tell you." Jason's breathing was definitely off-kilter, but he knew he had to proceed as planned.

"What?" Blue looked concerned. "Is this about Celia?"

He was gratified to see the disgusted

expression on Blue's face when she mentioned Celia. Where there was disgust, there was jealousy. Where there was jealousy . . . there was—possibly—love. "No . . . not directly. I mean, not at all."

Blue nodded thoughtfully. "So everything is good between you two." This wasn't a question; it was a statement.

"Yeah . . . well, no." He paused. "Actually we broke up today. I mean, *I* broke up with *her* today. It's finished." He had leaped the first hurdle.

"Jason . . . I'm sorry." Blue had moved from confusion to utter befuddlement. She obviously had no idea where this conversation was headed.

"Don't be." On the other side of the door someone pounded insistently.

"Dude, let me in!" a guy yelled. "My jacket's in there!"

Jason rolled his eyes. If he opened this door for one person, a stampede would begin. He had to be strong. Jason turned around and opened the door an inch. "Pick up your coat tomorrow, man. We're busy." Jason slammed the door shut and turned back to Blue.

"Jason, something is *definitely* wrong with you. You're acting like a total freak."

If he was ever going to say the words, now was the time. But how could he speak when he was hyperventilating? This was insanity, pure insanity. Blue could never love Jason the way he loved her. She was everything . . . and he was nothing.

Blue was sweet, intelligent, and beautiful. Jason was a generally depressed guy who had accidentally—stupidly—hit a little boy with his car when he was sixteen years old. *But you have to get past that,* Jason reminded himself. *Forgive yourself.* Somewhere deep inside he heard Dr. Grady's soothing voice. *Jason, you have to find a way to reconcile yourself with what happened two years ago and learn to live again.*

Blue stood up. "Jason, tell me what's going on." She reached out and clasped his bare forearm. "You're scaring me."

"I love you, Blue." He wasn't even sure he had said the words aloud.

Her face softened. "I love you, too—you know that."

He shook his head. This was the hardest thing he had ever done in his entire life. "No . . . I mean, I'm *in* love with you."

Her face was blank. He didn't see happiness or sadness or even shock. Just . . . nothing. "Blue?"

"I . . . I . . . I." She took a few steps backward and fell into the sofa. "I . . ."

He walked toward her. "Blue, *say* something." This was death. No, this was worse than death—it was like the most painful torture ever invented by some short, evil man with a heart of stone.

"Jason, I—" Behind him the door flew open.

And there was Christian Sands. As they said, timing was everything. "Hey, guys!" Christian said enthusiastically.

Jason's heart sank. The moment of truth was over—and Jason was no closer to knowing how Blue felt about him. Would the torture ever end?

## Dylan Talks to Females About the Relationship Between Girls and Sports

As a lot of you know, I have thankfully moved beyond those high school years during which guys have to define themselves in terms of what sport they do or do not play in any given season. It's only because I graduated from Alta Vista last spring, complete with several varsity letters and a headful of beautiful sports memories, that I can now address this subject with anything approaching honesty.

Here's the truth as I see it. Guys load themselves up with padding and helmets and drag themselves onto the football field in order to get pounded by anyone the slightest bit bigger than they are for one reason and one reason only. The chicks dig it.

Do you girls think we *enjoy* running around the track thirty times or staying at home on a Friday night so we're well rested at that Saturday morning soccer game? Do you think we enjoy those sweaty hours in the weight room or all the humiliating insults that are hurled back and forth in the locker room? No way!

We would all rather be at home watching *Wings* reruns and eating Ruffles and Eskimo Pie ice creams. We would rather be taking naps or reading magazines. But no, that's not a possibility. Why? Because girls—whether they be brains, or jocks, or artists—like the guy who scores the winning touchdown, run, or point in whatever sport is the talk of the school at any given time.

So don't say degrading things about us when we smell like pigs or seem mopey after the team loses the biggest game of the season. We're doing our pathetic best. And we're doing it for *you*.

Sam scanned the upper deck of the houseboat, astounded by just how many people had shown up tonight. He was way past beginning to regret the decision to throw a huge bash. He would probably be finding empty cans and crushed cigarette butts behind couches and under chairs for the rest of the summer.

"Yo, Bardin, check this out!" Guy Bennis yelled from the rail of the deck. He held a bottle rocket in one outstretched hand. "Get ready for a repeat of the Fourth of July!"

"Don't—" Sam screamed. Guy lit the bottle rocket with a small disposable lighter. A moment later the firework shot out of his hand and out over the water. "—light that," Sam finished.

He knew he should heave himself out of the lounge chair and go give Guy a lecture about fire hazards and city laws against anything even resembling an explosive, especially since he had already received at least half a dozen calls from angry neighbors. But his energy was drained. He maintained his position on the lounger and pretended that he had no idea that laws were being broken a mere twenty feet from his post.

Suddenly Eddie's head popped up from beneath the deck. Sam waved. "Over here," he called meekly.

Eddie climbed the last of the stairs and jogged to Sam's side. His hair was sticking out in a million directions, and his face was flushed. "Sam, some guy named Remo just puked all over my bed!"

"Lovely." Man, this whole scene was *way* out of control.

"What should I do?" Eddie asked. "My room reeks . . . and I don't even want to talk about what kind of chunks were floating in that guy's vomit."

"Uh . . ." Good question. What did one do in this type of situation? "Tell him to go outside if he's planning to do any more puking, then take the sheets off your bed. . . . We'll deal with it tomorrow."

"Okay." Eddie retreated.

Sam sighed. He certainly hoped that this Remo character had someone to drive him home—otherwise the guy might end up camped out on the Bardins' living-room sofa or (more likely) on the floor of the bathroom until morning. *Three, two, one.* Sam heaved himself up off the lounge chair. It was time he faced the reality of what was going on inside the houseboat—no matter how ugly that reality turned out to be.

Thank goodness for Dylan and Natalie. Both of them had taken on the role of host aide, and Sam knew they had done everything in their power to keep the party from becoming perilous. As always Sam found comfort in the knowledge that he had the love and support of two of the best people on earth. The thought was—perhaps—both cheesy and overly sentimental, but there was no denying its inherent truth. His friends meant everything to him.

Sam ignored the several guys who called his name as he plowed his way through the crowded deck. Man, there were a lot of guys here. The male-female ratio was probably four to one, and the girls seemed to be disappearing at a much faster rate than the guys. Which meant that a fistfight could break out at any minute.

Sam took the steps leading downstairs two at a time. He hadn't checked on Dylan for over an hour. It was entirely possible that he and Hallie were cuddled up somewhere sharing their life histories. As for Natalie . . . she was probably being hit on by every jerk at the party. It was time for the knight to rescue his damsel in distress.

Sam walked into the kitchen, which would probably qualify as a hazardous waste dump at this point. There were crushed cans everywhere, the floor was covered with dark red punch of some sort, and every dish the Bardins owned was out of the cabinets and littering the dirt-covered counters. "Oh, man . . ." He couldn't deal with this now.

Vanessa was sitting in front of the refrigerator, looking totally plastered. "Vanessa, have you seen Dylan or Natalie?"

She blinked at him. "That way. . . ." She waved her hand in the general direction of his bedroom.

"Thanks." Ooh. It was clear that Vanessa was going to have a nasty hangover in the morning. Sam had never understood the appeal of drinking oneself into a stupor, behaving like an idiot, and then feeling like an absolute wreck for forty-eight hours.

His bedroom door was closed. At first Sam didn't hear any noise from within. He was almost afraid to open the door—odds were that some couple was making use of the room to commit some unspeakable act. But then he heard giggling. Not just any giggling—Natalie's.

Sam grinned. She had probably decided to seek refuge from the chaos of the party at large. He didn't blame her. In fact, nothing sounded more tempting right now than hiding out with Natalie in his bedroom until every last straggler had taken their leave of the Bardin household. He couldn't wait for this ill-conceived night to be *over*.

He pushed open the door. "Hello, hello,

rescue nine-one-one is here to relieve you of—"

Sam stopped dead in his tracks. Natalie was in here, all right. But she wasn't alone. She was wrapped tightly in the arms of another guy. White-hot anger flowed through Sam's veins. He would kill the jerk!

Only the guy wasn't some nameless jerk. He was Dylan. "What . . ."

Suddenly Natalie looked up. "Sam!" she gasped.

"Sam . . . ," Dylan echoed.

"What the hell is going on here?" Sam shouted. He was hallucinating. He had to be. Neither Dylan nor Natalie would ever do something like this to him. The very idea was unthinkable.

"Sam . . . I—"

But there were lipstick marks on Dylan's face. Sam recognized the color—Clinique's Honey. It was Natalie's favorite. And Natalie's hair was a mess. Her long dark locks were full of tangles.

This simply couldn't happen right here, right now. In his bedroom. His world started to fade to black.

Natalie tore herself from Dylan's arms. *Oh, God. This is bad. This is very, very bad.* She wished the floor would open up and swallow her whole. A watery grave would be far more appealing than the scenario that was unfolding in front of her eyes. Sam looked like a ghost.

She rushed forward. "Sam, I can explain. . . ."

He held up his hands. "Don't come near me."

Natalie kept walking despite his warning. She needed to touch him. She needed to smooth the hurt from his face and somehow reverse time so that none of this had ever happened. "Sam, please." She reached out to put her hands on his shoulders.

"Don't touch me!" Sam screamed. His face had turned ashy white, then deep red. Now it was deepening to purple.

Dylan stepped forward. "Dude . . . this isn't what you think."

"It's not?" Sam shouted. "What is it, then? Please tell me." His whole body was trembling.

A deep sense of self-loathing crept through Natalie. This was so, so wrong. She was the worst person who had ever lived. "We were just . . ."

There was no way to finish that sentence. They were just—what? Giving each other mouth-to-mouth? Practicing wrestling moves? What could she say?

"I care about you so much, Sam." She felt tears welling up in her eyes. "We both do."

"We love you, man," Dylan said quietly. He looked completely destroyed. His eyes were darkened, and Natalie noticed that he looked much older than eighteen. He looked like an old man who just realized his life had been meaningless.

This was all her fault. Sam's heartbreak. Dylan's anguish. It was all her lousy fault. "Sam, I'm so sorry—"

"Just shut up," Sam said quietly. "Both of you make me sick."

So this was what her love for Dylan had led to. A mess. "Please don't say that, Sam. Please." Tears were streaming down Natalie's face now.

And even worse than her shame was the fact that she still had the memory of Dylan's kisses burning on her lips. Her body still tingled, and her head was still foggy from the feeling of his arms circling her body and hugging her close. Oh, God. She was still *happy*.

"Get out of my house," Sam said. His voice was devoid of emotion now. The stony look in his deep brown eyes was even worse than the anger that had blazed there just seconds ago. "I never want to see either of you again."

Natalie felt paralyzed. She couldn't take a step forward, and she couldn't take a step back. Time had frozen. For several moments no one made a move. Natalie felt like one of the wax figures in Madame Tussaud's museum.

"Sam!" Eddie had appeared at the bedroom door. "You have to come here *now!*"

They all stared at Eddie, the spell broken.

"What's wrong?" Natalie asked.

"Cops!" Eddie shouted. "The cops are here!"

"Jeez. . . ." Dylan started toward the door. "I'll go talk to them."

Sam blocked the door. "I don't need your help."

Panic swept over Natalie. "Come on, Sam. Now isn't the time—"

"I'll handle this myself." He glared at each of them in turn, then stalked out of the bedroom.

Natalie stared at his retreating back, wondering what it had all come to. She loved Sam . . . but she loved Dylan, too. And that was something she was going to have to face—no matter what the consequences.

Two blue-uniformed police officers stood at the door of the Bardins' houseboat. Sam glanced at each of their badges, forcing his mind away from the scene in his bedroom. This was a crisis that couldn't wait.

"Hello, Officers," Sam said affably. "How can I help you?"

"Where are your parents?" the one on the left asked. His name was D. Fineman, and he looked like he could easily bench-press a couple hundred pounds.

"They're not here," Sam said (pleasantly, he hoped).

The officer on the right—P. Griane—grunted. "Where are they?"

There was no good answer to that question. "My mother and father are currently . . . indisposed," Sam said. He had learned through experience that the word *indisposed* covered just about every unpleasant task with which a person could possibly be engaged.

"Do either of them *live* here?" P. Griane asked.

"No . . . not right now." The pain of every horrible thing in Sam's life seemed highlighted by that one statement.

D. Fineman glanced over Sam's shoulder. "We were told that underage kids are drinking alcoholic beverages here tonight."

"No, sir. Not here." *Lie, lie, lie.* "No one in here is drinking. We're just having good, clean fun." *Except for the fact that my girlfriend and my best friend were making out in my very own bedroom,* he added silently.

Guy Bennis suddenly appeared at Sam's side. "Dude, we're out of beer." He punched Sam on the shoulder. "We've got to find someone with a good fake ID to go on a booze run."

Terrific. Sam figured he might as well take Officer P. Griane's gun out of its holster and shoot himself in the head on the spot. He had a feeling that this little cop-civilian interchange was about to take a nasty turn.

"Are you the person in charge here?" D. Fineman asked.

"Uh . . . I guess so." Sam knew that had been a trick question, but unfortunately there was no one else to lay the blame on.

"Are you aware of the fact that a Mr. Kevin Marlin just received a DUI citation as he was traveling from this location to his own residence?"

Uh-oh. These guys weren't just here to tell Sam to keep down the music or to break up the party. They meant serious business. "No, sir . . . I mean, I didn't even know half the people who were here tonight."

Eddie tugged on the sleeve of Sam's denim shirt. "Are we in trouble?" he asked.

Officer P. Griane stared down at Eddie. "Trouble doesn't even begin to describe it," he said ominously.

"I'll tell everyone to leave right away," Sam said quickly. "I mean, I didn't *know* anyone here was drinking. I specifically said that no one was allowed to consume alcohol under my roof. . . ."

Sam wondered if this was what his father had felt as he lied to cops, prosecutors, and judges during his arrest and trial. At this moment he knew that he would tell any lie in order to get these cops to walk back to their squad car and drive away. He wanted the whole situation to disappear.

From far inside the houseboat Sam heard a retching sound. He didn't have to look inside to know who was puking. Vanessa Elison was tossing her cookies all over the linoleum floor of the kitchen. "Anyway, thanks for coming by," he said to the cops. "I'll be sure to get this situation under control immediately." *I'll also be sure to kick Dylan O'Connor's butt from here to Los Angeles just as soon as you get out of my face.*

"What's your name, son?" Officer Fineman asked.

Sam's stomach twisted into a tight, painful knot. "Samuel Bardin," he answered.

Officer Griane stepped forward, holding out a pair of gray steel handcuffs. "Samuel Bardin, you are under arrest. You have the right to remain silent. Anything you say can and will be held against you in a court of law. You have the right to an attorney. . . ."

As the officer continued to recite Sam his Miranda rights, Sam felt the cold metal of the handcuffs close around his wrists. The policeman's voice became indistinguishable from the roaring in Sam's ears. He was being carted off to jail—like father, like son.

D. Fineman clasped Sam's shoulders and began to guide him toward the squad car that was parked on the street. Behind him Sam was aware of the fact that Eddie, Dylan, and Natalie were looking on in horror.

Sam looked over his shoulder. "Call Dad's lawyer!" he yelled to Eddie. Then he glanced at Dylan and Natalie. "And both of you get the hell out of my house!"

Sam was dimly aware of the fact that he was screaming. But the sound of his own voice was muffled by the avalanche of emotions that were coursing through him. His world had, at last, collapsed. And he was going to jail.

Sam had finally done it. He had sunk as low as his parents. And he didn't know if he would ever find a way out of this deep black hole. Even worse, he didn't know if he wanted to. . . .

## A Dark Night in the City

**EPILOGUE**

*The hour was 2:00 A.M. Fog had rolled into San Francisco, covering the city in a blanket of white-gray haze. The air was chilly . . . daylight seemed a lifetime away. Throughout the Bay Area, employees of @café were alone with their thoughts, their feelings, and their worries. . . .*

Natalie van Lenton sat silent and alone, gazing out of her bedroom window. Even though she had donned her favorite flannel pajamas and wrapped herself in the fluffy down comforter from her bed, she couldn't shake the feeling of extreme uneasiness that had descended on her as she watched Sam disappear into that patrol car. Her thoughts were a miserable, jumbled mess.

Natalie played out the night's events in her mind, her mood swinging wildly from ecstasy to desolation as she thought first of Dylan's kisses and then of Sam's arrest. Kisses. Arrest. Kisses. Arrest.

Natalie pushed herself off her chaise longue and headed back to

177

her bed. If only there were something she could do for Sam—call a lawyer, post bail, send him a cake with a razor baked inside—anything. But Dylan and Eddie were taking care of all the ugly business that was associated with getting arrested—there was no role for her now that she had flubbed the part of supportive girlfriend.

Natalie flopped onto her bed. She was useless. Depressed, useless . . . and perhaps worst of all, still madly in love with Dylan O'Connor.

Sam Bardin stared at the gray cement walls of the small holding cell into which he had been unceremoniously thrust and prayed for morning. Never, never, never had he been so humiliated.

Up until the moment when a poker-faced policewoman had shoved his fingers into a pad of black ink, Sam had thought that the cops were going to let him off with a stern lecture and warning. But no, they had to prove a point about minors and drinking. And Sam—son of a convicted felon—was going to be their poster boy. Peachy.

Sam tentatively lay down on the thin pallet these people called a bed. At least he was alone in the cell. There wasn't some huge ex-wrestler named Bubba staring at him with who knew what in his eyes. Sam was left to ponder the absolute ruin of his life in isolation.

*Natalie.* How could she have done that to him? How could Dylan have done it? There was simply no answer. Had Sam been arrested a week ago or even a day ago, he would have been bummed. Hell, he would have hated himself for setting such a bad example for Eddie. But he wouldn't have experienced the desperate sense of loneliness that he felt now.

Because when Sam got sprung from this joint tomorrow morning, he wasn't going to walk out into the sun and into the loving arms of his two best friends in the world. Nope. As of this moment he was starting his life over again—and he was going to have absolutely nothing to do with anyone or anything associated with Natalie, Dylan, or the damn café.

Tanya Childes was a creature of impulse. Her style was act, *then* think. But not this night, this time, this situation. Major was too important to be approached when her mood had just completed a one-eighty. She needed time to digest the night's events . . . and to think.

She sat crossed-legged on the floor of her bedroom, taking deep, even breaths. Thank goodness for the yoga meditation tape her mom had put in her room a few days ago. These relaxation exercises felt like a gift from God. Tanya focused her thoughts and continued to breathe. *If*

*Major loves me, that will be wonderful.* In. *If Major doesn't love me, I will survive.* Out.

Tanya had learned something tonight. She had learned that she, Tanya Childes, serial dater extraordinaire, could go to a party by herself. And she could leave by herself. No bolt of lightning flashed from the sky and struck her dead because she didn't flirt with every halfway cute guy at the party. She could be alone . . . and that was okay. It was better than okay. Being an independent woman who didn't need the drunken, shallow approval of some hormonally overloaded teenage male felt *good.*

*I can be alone.* In. *I don't need a guy to make me feel like a valuable person.* Out. In. Out. Tanya opened her eyes. She was very tired suddenly.

Tanya untangled her legs and stood up. Tonight she would sleep peacefully. And tomorrow . . . tomorrow she would see what the day had to offer. Good or bad, she could handle it.

Jason Kirk sat at the edge of the water, gazing up at the fog that lay low over the Pacific Ocean. Any normal person would be feeling very cold right now. The temperature had dropped to forty degrees, and the wind had picked up considerably. But he was sweating.

"Did I really tell Blue that I'm in love with her?" he asked a small sand crab that was working its way out of a hole in the sand. "Did I really rip out my heart and hand it to Blue on a silver platter?"

The sand crab didn't seem interested in Jason's question. Neither did the small waves that lapped at his feet. But Jason knew from his pounding heart that he had indeed taken the plunge. He searched his soul for pangs of regret, humiliation, or profound disillusionment with the world. But he found none of those things. Instead Jason found something that resembled contentment.

"The truth will set you free," he told the sand crab. Sure, Jason knew in his heart that there was no possible way Blue could ever return his feelings. And he knew that now their friendship could never be the same.

But finally he had found his voice. And he had used it. From now on Jason didn't have to hide from his feelings—he was, in a word, free. *The truth will set you free.* . . . Yes, the truth was everything. And he was never again going to forget that. No matter what the price.

Dylan O'Connor drove through the empty streets of San Francisco. As soon as Sam had been taken away in the police car, he and Eddie had jumped into the Oldsmobile and driven to the police station. They had been informed by a dour-faced lieutenant that bail couldn't be posted until morning. Sam was spending the night in jail, and there was nothing Dylan could do to change that fact.

But there was plenty he could have done to change other facts in Sam's life. For starters, Dylan could have refrained from making out with his best friend's girlfriend in the middle of said best friend's bedroom. Dylan also should have known that Sam's party was a recipe for disaster from the beginning and done everything in his power to stop the thing from ever taking place. Unfortunately Dylan had been too weak to look out for anyone's interests but his own. He had practically held Sam's hand and guided him down a path toward destruction.

Dylan wanted to be a good, kind person who followed the Golden Rule and led a basically sin-free life. He wanted to be worthy of love, and admiration, and trust. But he also wanted Natalie van Lenton so badly that it made him ache. He turned onto Sheridan Avenue.

The van Lentons' home was a mere half block away. If Dylan kept driving, he would prove to himself that he was headed down the road that would eventually lead to something like righteousness. If he stopped, he would know that he was a guy who was more than a little selfish.

The car kept moving, the house got closer and closer, and still Dylan had no idea what he was going to do. . . .

Blue O'Connor was still wearing the dress she had chosen for Sam's party. The thought of putting on a T-shirt and slipping into bed was laughable. Sleep had never seemed so far away. She had settled herself on her beanbag chair, opened a bag of Doritos, and begun to rhythmically crunch her way through the bag.

Tonight had been . . . everything. Horrible, wonderful, awkward, thrilling—everything. She still couldn't believe that Jason had said what he had said. The whole scene had blown her away. She also couldn't believe how Christian had reacted to her silence in the car on the way home. He had grilled her for almost half an hour about what she and Jason had been talking about. And the more Blue insisted that they had simply been chewing the fat, the more determined Christian had become to discover *exactly* what words had been exchanged.

Blue had never felt so . . . cherished. The idea that a guy could be jealous over her was mind-blowing. And her reaction to Christian's macho routine had been the craziest of all.

She had kissed him. Not a peck-on-the-lips kiss. A real, passionate kiss. And she had loved it. When their lips finally parted, Christian had gazed searchingly into her eyes.

"I don't know what's going on between you and

Jason," he had said. "But I know that I like you more than I've ever liked another girl. And I need to know whether or not you feel the same way about me."

He had paused, and in that moment Blue had felt that her heart was going to explode out of her chest and land on the windshield of his Jeep. "When you figure out what you want to say to me, give me a call. I'll be waiting."

Now it was hours later. And Blue had decided what it was she needed to say to the guy she loved. Blue leaned over and picked up the phone. She had to make this call tonight. The rest of her life couldn't wait until morning.

## About the Author

Elizabeth Craft is the author of many young adult novels, but *@café* is her first very own series. Ms. Craft is originally from Kansas City. Currently, she lives in a tiny studio apartment in New York's Greenwich Village. She enjoys reading romance novels, going to bad movies, and cruising coffee shops for cute guys.

# You love the TV show, now you can read the books!

## A brand-new book series

### #1 Everybody Say Moesha!
Can Mo keep her love classified?
01147-2/$3.99

### #2 Keeping It Real
Mo's boyfriend's got it going on.
But has he got something going on the side?
01148-0/$3.99

### #3 Trippin' Out
Is trippin' to NYC going to be trouble?
01149-9/$3.99

### #4 Hollywood Hook-Up
Is Hakeem the mack - or is he whack?
01151-0/$3.99

 Available from Archway Paperbacks
Published by Pocket Books

**Simon & Schuster Mail Order**
**200 Old Tappan Rd., Old Tappan, N.J. 07675**
Please send me the books I have checked above. I am enclosing $_____ (please add $0.75 to cover the postage and handling for each order. Please add appropriate sales tax). Send check or money order--no cash or C.O.D.'s please. Allow up to six weeks for delivery. For purchase over $10.00 you may use VISA: card number, expiration date and customer signature must be included.

POCKET
BOOKS

Name _____

Address _____

City _____ State/Zip _____

VISA Card # _____ Exp.Date _____

Signature _____

1358-03

TM & © 1997 Big Ticket Television Inc. All rights reserved.